THE ROYAL TRADE

A BILLIONAIRE PRINCE ROMANCE

ERIN HAYES

ERIN HAYES BOOKS

THE ROYAL TRADE:
A Billionaire Prince Romance
by Erin Hayes

This is a work of fiction. Names, characters, organizations, places, events, and incidences are either products of the author's imagination or used fictitiously.

Copyright © 2016 Erin Hayes

Cover by The Book Brander
Editing by Lindsay Galloway of Contagious Edits

No part of this book may be reproduced or stored in a retrieval system or transmitted in any form by any means, electronic, mechanical, photocopying, recording, or otherwise, without express written permission of the publisher.

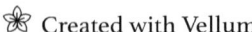 Created with Vellum

For Lindsay who has been an absolute saint throughout this whole book, and who probably appreciates the New Zealand parts of this book as much as I do.

PROLOGUE
CARA

*7*01...709...719...727...733...739...

In my head, I count all the prime numbers in order, an old habit that calms me when I'm nervous or panicked or otherwise freaked out.

Oh, yeah, I'm totally freaked out right now.

Because this is Monarch's Day, the day that a small island in the Mediterranean Sea became a country six hundred years ago. It seems like the world's aristocrats and bureaucrats and diplomats have gathered to celebrate at the annual ball. The Dubrevian palace has turned into an exclusive venue with glamorous decorations, a full orchestra, red carpets, and dancing water fountains. I think I saw a flock of swans somewhere near the bathrooms.

Dubreva may be a small player on the global stage, but they throw parties like no one else. Cameras and reporters have swarmed the palace, there are so many people here I don't know, and I'm afraid of insulting a president and causing World War III.

Who would have ever thought a math nerd from Missouri would end up here?

743...751...757...761...

Oh my god.

I'll probably get to $2^{74,207,281}-1$, the highest known prime number, by the end of the night. I keep checking the time and it seems to be going oh so slowly. I smile and try to look as gracious as possible.

All this glitz and glam isn't my kind of scene. I wish I could just curl up with my Kindle and read until two in the morning. Like I used to before I met my boyfriend.

Here, my boyfriend, Crown Prince Phillip Celestro di'Vale of Dubreva, is in his element. He soaks it up like a lizard in the sun, talking and rubbing elbows with nobles. I'd been staying by his side, using him as a shield to ward off any prying questions or comments. Phillip warned me that some reporters may try to find a scandal to write about for the paper in the morning. They've been especially cruel to me, as an American dating a handsome billionaire prince, accusing me of being a gold digger.

Things like that are why I like to stay away from these kinds of events. Less of a stage for me to fuck up.

Yet, I've lost Phillip in the sea of ball gowns and $20,000 tuxedos. Hence my panic.

769…773…787…797…

"Cara! Well aren't you a vision of sophistication!" an elderly woman with a fur boa exclaims in a thick, unrecognizable accent. She's holding one of those long cigarette holders and gives me two air kisses for each cheek.

I have no idea who this woman is. But I smile and nod graciously.

"Thank you," I say, bobbing my head (but not too far, as Phillip warned me. As it's Dubreva's celebration, if I curtsey too far, it could be seen as a sign of weakness). "You look lovely yourself."

"Oh, this old thing?" The woman does a slow turn, and the rhinestones embedded in her dress glitter blindingly. "I figured I should wear a favorite, this being Dubreva's six hundredth anniversary."

"It's very pretty," I say, not knowing what else to say. I doubt she'd be interested in discussing whether the *abc* conjecture was solved in 2012. I've been studying the four papers online and it's fascinating. At least for me.

The woman nods and walks away. Apparently, I didn't meet her standards.

I let out a disappointed breath. There's no way I'll be able to make it through tonight. And, I've just realized that I've lost my place in counting prime numbers.

2…3…5…7…

"Here."

A whiskey glass is shoved into my hands, filled with an amber liquid and crystal clear ice cubes. I look up to see Phillip's younger brother, Eric, winking at me. His bow tie is loose and his dark hair is disheveled, giving him a roguish appearance, even in his tux.

He salutes me with his own glass. "You have to drink, or else you'll never make it through these events." He's apparently been taking his own advice to heart, and his speech is slurred.

I think the drink is scotch, and I feel the sudden compulsion to chug the whole thing. I throw it back, grimacing as the liquid hits my gullet. I cover my mouth with the back of my hand, hoping that no one sees me unable to hold down my liquor.

"Thank you," I cough.

Eric's eyebrows raise in surprise. "Wow, I was thinking you'd be sipping on that for a while, but I guess that will do as well. You apparently needed it."

I nod and put on a brave smile. "These events are a little hard on me," I admit. "I don't fit in here at all."

Eric nods. "Try doing these your whole life."

I cross my arms, and look across the room to see Phillip laughing it up with a group of diplomats from Thailand. He's smiling, completely in his element here.

"Your brother seems to enjoy them."

Eric shakes his head with a roll of his eyes. "No, Phillip *has* to enjoy them. There's a difference."

"How would you rather spend your time?" I ask him. At least while I'm talking to the younger prince of Dubreva, I'm not left by myself.

Eric shrugs, an easy smile on his face. "Well, between driving my valet absolutely batty and getting out of the country every chance I get, I like getting to know the natives better wherever I am." He winks at me.

I let out a laugh, feeling my cheeks turn red. "Right. I could have guessed that."

Eric has the reputation for being quite the playboy. Every other weekend, he's in the tabloids with another scorned lover. Or he's partying naked in Las Vegas. That happened a few weeks ago, much to their mother's dismay.

"What are the girls like back home in Missouri," he asks suddenly, his expression serious. "Are they all like you?"

I look at him, wondering what he's getting at. I give him a thin-lipped smile, trying to keep myself from looking too far into his words. "They're probably just as nervous as I am right now. The Kansas City Chiefs are playing in the NFL Playoffs."

He watches me for a moment, his eyes intense, before he smirks and sips on his scotch. "Well, we could use more like you at this party."

I nod, still not getting what he's saying, but that could be because he's drunk. "How's the lap?" I ask, bringing up an old joke. The first time I met him, I spilled soup in his lap. Long story. I was counting prime numbers that day too.

He pauses before answering. "Everything's in working order, if that's what you're asking."

"I still feel guilty about that."

He gives me a strange look. "Don't."

"There you are, Cara!"

We both turn to see Phillip running up to us. I

smile at my boyfriend, feeling my entire face light up. "Hey love," I say.

"Is my brother making trouble for you?" Phillip asks, giving Eric a mock disapproving glare.

Eric shrugs. "I've just been making her more comfortable," he says. "Poor thing was nowhere near drunk enough for this kind of party."

Phillip rolls his eyes and entwines his fingers in mine. "Come on," he whispers in my ear. "We need to make our way to the dais. Mother is going to make some announcements for the party and I want you there."

Their mother doesn't like me very much, but the fact that she wants me to be a part of this means that she's at least accepted me now.

"Sorry to abandon you like this, Eric," I tell him.

"No worries," Eric says, saluting with his drink. "I'll go see if I can find a single baroness."

Phillip sighs and leads me away. "I swear, my brother..." he mutters under his breath. "Sorry if he did anything untoward."

I close my eyes, the scent of him filling my head. I have no idea how Phillip does it—he always smells both exotic and woodsy, no matter if we're on the beach or lying in bed or showering. Or at an event like this. He makes this whole ordeal bearable.

"Are you enjoying yourself?" Phillip asks.

"Mostly," I admit.

"Sorry, I got pulled away by the royal family of Sweden." He lets out a breath. "They wanted to talk about some sort of Summit."

"It's all right. I know this is basically work for you."

"No excuse. I won't leave your side the rest of the night, I promise." Phillip stops and gives me a kiss. It's chaste by anyone's standards, but it has to be in such a public space. Still though, it warms me all the way to my toes.

I love him. He is my 3/5 to my 2/5 to make one whole.

We've been together for four years, ever since we met at Oxford University. Four years of wonderful bliss. Even though we come from entirely different worlds, he treats me like a princess. Something I never dreamed possible.

His mother is waiting for us near the dais. Her white hair piled on her head and she's wearing a purple dress, looking every bit like the elegant queen she is. She used to intimidate me every time I talked with her, but she's warmed up to me in the past few months.

She gives me a smile. "I hope you're enjoying the Monarch's Day Ball, Cara," she says.

"I am, your grace," I say, dropping into a curtsey. I still haven't mastered those yet.

Victoria's eyes soften just the slightest bit. "Good." She glances at her son. "Phillip, are you ready?"

He swallows and nods. "Yes."

Is he nervous?

Phillip has my hand gripped firmly in his as he leads me up the steps to the dais to address the entire party. Here, I see just how many people are here for the ball—probably three hundred. No wonder I feel like I am out of my league.

I blink several times as flashes from cameras assault me at various intervals. Oh my, this is such a big event for the country.

I start my prime number counting again as the Prime Minister of Dubreva thanks everyone for celebrating the country's Monarch's Day. At one point, the orchestra plays the Dubrevian national anthem and I stand to attention, listening to it. There is applause at points during speeches and I clap along with them, but I can't help the flip-flopping of my stomach as I stand up here. I'm nervous myself, and it's a different kind of nervousness than stage fright.

I get the first hint when Phillip takes the center stage. He's so handsome as he exudes confidence for the entire crowd. He commands them like a ship's captain. Everyone hangs onto his every word. I know, because I'm doing the same.

At least, I think I do. Because he drops to one knee in front of me, holding out a little black box for me. I watch him, confusedly, before I realize what it's for. I look down and see the glittering diamond engagement ring.

"Oh my god," I whisper as the entire crowd laughs at my reaction. Here, in such a public place? This is not how I imagined this would happen. Certainly in a more private way.

Here, I feel oddly exposed.

"Cara Marie Van Meter," Phillip says. "You've made my life wonderful for the past four years. You bring me joy, you challenge me, you make me a better man. And I want to keep this going for the rest of my life. So, Cara Marie Van Meter—will you marry me?"

I gulp down air as my vision tunnels. My knees lock and I nearly faint. Nearly, though.

I look out over the crowd again, because I don't know where to look. And, despite how packed the ballroom is, I see him. Eric. Moving around the back.

His eyes are on the stage, a deep frown on his face. The intensity of his gaze is a tempest, sucking my attention towards him.

He's...*angry*?

And, for the life of me, I can't figure out why.

I give myself a slight shake and look back down at Phillip, who is grinning up at me, hope spreading across his face. My boyfriend, prince of my heart, and prince of a beautiful country. I love him.

And I know for sure he loves me.

"Yes," I tell Phillip, finally allowing the smile to blossom. "I do. I will marry you, my prince."

Phillip rises to his feet and kisses me to the applause of the crowd.

Fairy tales do come true. And this is the start of my happily ever after.

1

CARA

"Cara," Suzi, my best friend since kindergarten, whispers to me with a well-placed elbow to my ribs. "The news."

I'm with all my girlfriends at a restaurant in Venice. We're in the middle of my bachelorette party, living up life before I'm set to marry Phillip in a few weeks.

"What?" I ask around a mouthful of spaghetti.

"The news," Angela says. "You, uh, should watch this."

I swivel around in my seat to look at the screen. Why there is a TV in a restaurant like this, I'll never know. In such an ancient city, it seems so out of place. I turn towards it, spaghetti practically falling out of my mouth. At first, with the flashing red lights and darkened street in Paris, I think there's something awful happening. Like a terrorist attack or some sort of assassination.

Thankfully, it's none of that.

Just my fiancée leaving a hotel off Champs Elysees. I'm an American and have been to Paris only once (with my fiancée, of course), so my knowledge of the city is very limited, but I do recognize the area right away. And I recognize Phillip's "fuck off" expression as he ducks into a limo with a beautiful brunette while snaps from paparazzi flash every second. The red police lights are from the security details.

My stomach drops, as does the spaghetti from my mouth. I don't even care as the pasta falls in my lap. No one else cares right now either.

"Can you turn it up?" I feebly ask the restaurant owner in English. My friend Giorgia says something to him in Italian and he obliges.

Of course, the entire newsfeed is in Italian, so I'm only watching images.

"What's happening?" I ask Giorgia.

The woman's face tightens into a frown. "They're…saying things, Cara."

"What kind of things?"

Giorgia exchanges glances with Suzi, and somehow, my friend from St. Louis who doesn't speak a lick of Italian understands before I do. Her face is white and she gives me a sick look.

"They're saying that Phillip has been caught cheating," Giorgia translates.

I shake my head. Even though I saw her on screen with him, it still doesn't register. Phillip loves me. We went to Oxford together. I moved halfway around the world for him. I love him back.

He *can't* be cheating on me.

The entire restaurant is quiet as everyone watches the news. It's like they know who I am. And they certainly know who he is.

There's no denying it—the screen shows snapshots of them around Paris. At first, the photostream starts off innocent, hanging out together or laughing. Then they're hugging, he has his arm around her. And the *crème de la crème*. A photo of them kissing. Followed by another one. And another one.

He's cheating on me.

I get up from my seat and run to the bathroom where I vomit up my spaghetti bolognese.

2

ERIC

The blonde makes sure to bend over in a way that I'm sure has turned a lot of other men's heads as she puts on her boots. They're Louboutin, made from the finest leather with their signature red soles. I recognize the brand because I've bought those shoes before for plenty of women—it's one surefire way of making them fall into bed with me.

She watches me coyly, giving me a smile as she slowly zips one boot up her calf. I watch her from the edge of the bed, with the white sheets across my naked lap. She's beautiful in a classic, Grace Kelly way; perfect body, great in bed, and if I remember correctly after the one-too-many-drinks I had last night, she even has a great sense of humor.

But as I watch her get ready to leave my hotel room, I feel...nothing.

She's not *her*. This blonde isn't the redheaded American that has captivated my every thought for years now.

"So..." the blonde says in a thick Italian accent, and I realize that I don't even remember her name. Am I that much of a pig that I stick my dick in anything that gives me the smallest hint of attention?

Apparently, yes.

She looks at me, a mirror of so many other girls before her. They're always hoping that this is the start of something between us. Fortune. Fame. Monarchy. They're hoping to grab their happily ever after any way they can.

I close my eyes and pinch the bridge of my nose. "Herbert will have you sign a nondisclosure agreement when you leave," I tell her. I can trust my valet to take care of her and make sure that our relationship doesn't extend beyond my hotel door.

The angry flush comes to her cheeks as she realizes what I'm insinuating.

"You..." she says, her voice lowering to dangerous levels. I'm not afraid of her. If anything, I feel incredibly sorry for her. For breaking her heart. For not being able to give her mine.

I know what that feels like. And that's exactly why I can't do anything more with her.

"Take last night for what it was," I say, flashing her what I know is a dashing smile. Even angry at me, I see her melt. "It's just a fond memory with the second-in-line to the Dubreva throne."

"But—" she starts.

The door opens and my valet, Herbert, comes in with his usual, detached manner. "Come, my lady. We'll see to it that you get back home safely."

The blonde lets out a genuine growl and glares at me as Herbert leads her from my room. I don't miss the disparaging glance the old man gives me in the doorway, before I'm left alone in my suite.

I fall backwards on the incredibly soft mattress and sigh heavily.

What should I do now?

Go home to Dubreva and stop being a fucking creep.

Yeah, that's *exactly* what I should do. But I don't get up from the bed.

Instead, I look out the window and see the lagoon.

It's no coincidence that I'm in Venice the same weekend that *she* is in Venice for her bachelorette party. Oh, trust me, I know what I've been doing this whole time. I was hoping to bump into her and talk with her. See her innocent, goofy smile. Maybe try to make her see something more in me.

So stupid.

Except I can't get her out of my mind. And one of the best and worst things is to have a private jet when you're trying not to stalk someone. What's more, I know where she's staying. I know the general idea of what she's doing, except one of the most beautiful things about her is her spontaneity. Such as last night when she was supposed to go to a play at one of the theatres, but she didn't. I suspect she got held up watching the sun set over the old city. She likes relax and get distracted by nature.

I'm talking about Cara Van Meter. A beautiful woman, clueless to how beautiful she is, and fiancée to my brother, the crown prince of Dubreva. They've been together for four years now. Four years.

But I was the one who saw her first.

I groan and roll on my side to grab my boxers off the floor. I put them on, more for decorum than modesty.

I need something to fill my thoughts, something to ease this hole I have in my chest. I grab the remote and flick the television on. Years of tutors and private schools have taught me to be fluent in six languages, including Italian, so I understand all the commercials and soap operas as I flip through the channels, trying to find something to interest me.

At first, I watch it with disinterest, switching between the channels as I try to find something that catches my fancy.

Then something does.

I sit up in the bed, watching in disbelief as I see my brother on the screen with a woman on his arm. And it's not Cara. It's some other woman, who is grinning. Phillip looks happy, she looks happy.

And I can imagine one person who is not happy at all.

I look out the window again, wondering where she is and if she's seen it yet.

Fuck, I hope not. Cara will be heartbroken when she finds out, and I want her to have just another moment thinking that my brother isn't an asshole.

Because, clearly, he is.

The thought makes me spring to my feet, and I pad to the balcony and lean against the railing. I'm in the Dogaressa Suite at the Belmond Hotel Cipriani. Detached from the main part of the city, but so damn close, I can almost smell her on the breeze.

I close my eyes and sigh.

She's most likely found out. She's probably crushed and crying. Wondering if she should go back to Dubreva to see Phillip, or back home to America to stay with her family.

Either way, there is stark reality facing her when she leaves Venice.

I clench my hands, and I realize that I've already made a decision even before I knew there was one to make.

Damn it. I'm about to get myself into trouble.

"Well, she was a fiery one, wasn't she?"

I turn to see Herbert behind me. He looks a little ruffled, and it takes me a moment to realize that he's not talking about Cara; he's talking about Miss Blonde What's-Her-Name. He straightens his coat and smooths his white hair back.

"I don't even remember her name," I murmur.

"Yes, well, I have the signed NDA papers that say she's a Miss Patrizia Giordani. And she's thirty-six years old and—"

"Really, she's thirty-six? I had her pegged at twenty-four." She's certainly as flexible as a girl in her early twenties.

"—and she's now heading back home via a water taxi," Herbert continues, ignoring my comment. "I wish you wouldn't dismiss your liaisons like that, sir.

One of these days, you're going to make the wrong choice, and—"

"They've all been the wrong choice, Herbert. Because they're not the right one."

Herbert presses his lips into a fine line, and I can tell that he's holding his tongue. He knows about my...*fixation*...on Cara and fully believes that I need to stop it.

I've tried. Miss I've-Forgotten-Her-Name-Again is testament to that.

I sigh and comb a hand through my coarse, dark hair. No matter how much I try to tame it, my ancient Greek roots take hold of my genes and gives me the appearance that I've just gotten out of bed.

The media loves it.

"Sir," Herbert says gently. "If I may say something?"

I raise an eyebrow. "You may."

Herbert clears his throat before speaking. "'Tough shit' as the youth like to say these days. You know she's spoken for. You know there is no chance."

I grin. "See, that's where you're wrong Herbert."

He catches my playful tone and groans. "Oh no, what have you concocted this time?"

"*I* haven't done anything," I tell him pointedly as

I cross the room. "It's what Phillip's done. Or rather, *who* he has done."

Herbert is unperturbed. "I sense you're still going to do something you'll regret."

"I'll regret it if I don't say something to her. Not when I have the chance"

I walk over to my wardrobe and start pulling out pressed shirts. Herbert hovers over me, but he learned a long time ago to let me do my own thing when I'm like this. When we're in Dubreva, fine, he can dress me. But when I'm out in the real world, I can take care of myself.

"Don't you think that poor girl has been hurt enough for one day?" Herbert's fingers drum on the side table. "Don't you think she needs some time to mourn?"

"And risk losing her forever?" I know her. She'll go back to America, hide, find some other bloke who will probably treat her like a princess. She deserves that.

I know that. I know it and damn it all.

I have to tell her. *Everything.* And then she can take my heart and do as she pleases with it. But for now, I just need to cling on to something akin to hope.

For my own sanity.

"What were you thinking, sir?" Herbert asks slowly.

I tug on my sports jacket and take out my phone to call her. "We're going to catch her before she leaves."

3

CARA

It's amazing how the world can go about its business when you're crumbling inside. I stand in front of the departures board at the Venice Marco Polo Airport, tears streaming down my face as I clutch my lone bag to my chest. People pass me, looking at me like I'm some sort of crazy woman.

I may very well be.

2…3…5…7…11…13…17…

After leaving the restaurant, I packed my bag and I immediately went to the airport. I know I left Suzi and Giorgia and the others in a bind, but I also don't want to cut their vacation in Venice short. Sure, they protested, saying that I should forget everything and enjoy myself on his billionaire dime.

But this was supposed to be my bachelorette party in one of the most romantic cities in the world. And I was never good at pretending to be happy when I feel like the world is ending.

I haven't booked a flight yet because I don't know what to do. Representatives from the Dubreva monarchy have called my cell every five minutes since the news hit the air. I can tell by the international code. None of them have been Phillip, which is the main reason for my silence.

I guess that says everything I need to know about where I stand in his eyes. The betrayal chokes me in the back of my throat.

Where should I go? Fly back to Dubreva? I know I probably have a million things I need to do there to clean up this mess. What even happens when a royal breaks off an engagement? I know I'm not a princess or anything, but I have so many things that were gifted to me as the royal consort.

I don't want that stuff. Not anymore. I guess I'll return it. Or donate it to charity.

Should I visit my friend Christabel in London to stay in Europe and see if Phillip ever wants to get ahold of me? Or go home to Missouri and hide under the covers, wishing that I had never heard of the Kingdom of Dubreva?

Indecision roots me to the spot, and I honestly don't know which is the better choice. I can see Phillip's mother fretting about their public image, her son, and even my own wellbeing, and I can't face her right now.

Home? Springfield hasn't been home for a long time, but it looks like it's my best option. Mom and Dad will lecture me, of course, about how foolish I was to fall in love with a prince and pretend like I was going to be a princess for a hot second. That will be unbearable.

At least the paparazzi won't get me there.

Then I realize...

Shit.

All I have on me is the American Express Black Card that Phillip gave me for expenses. It's been my lifeline for a few years now. I used it to book everything on this trip. I have my old Mastercard from when I was an undergrad, but I think the limit on it is $1,000 and I'm pretty sure that a last-minute flight will cost a lot more than that.

Shit, when did I start becoming so dependent on him? The thought sickens me as I blink furiously, trying to keep another set of tears at bay. I've become someone I don't even recognize anymore.

127...131...137...139...

Fuck it, I'll just pay him back once I get a job as a math professor, of course, like I had originally planned on when I started my graduate studies at Oxford University.

Where I met Phillip. Where I gave up my dreams to become the girlfriend of a prince. Who I thought was *my* prince.

Has he even tried calling me?

I blink furiously as I fish out my phone and snicker softly when I realize that this iPhone was a gift from Phillip as well. Oh my, how things are going to change drastically for me.

My notifications have blown up in the last two hours, and I grit my teeth as I scroll to the last phone call, marked as a Dubrevian number by its international code, +397.

Another prime number.

The thought brings the barest of smiles to my lips, even though Phillip hasn't tried calling me once. It hurts. And I try to hold in the tears, but it's so damn hard. It's a betrayal, confirmation of what he's done.

I'm not sure I can take this.

My phone rings, surprising me so much, I nearly drop it. Luckily, I'm able to hit the call-button and bring it to my ear.

"H—hello?"

"*Cara?!*"

I blink, the familiar voice slamming through my grief.

"E...*Eric?*"

Why the hell would Phillip's younger brother be calling me? I've had a few interactions with Eric, but nothing big. Well, aside from our first meeting when I spilled soup on his lap. That was even before I met Phillip, a complete coincidence.

Maybe...

A sinking feeling hits my stomach, and I wonder if this is Phillip trying to talk to me through his younger brother. Maybe Eric is going to tell me how it's over with Phillip and give me all the, "It's him, not you" shit that his brother told him to say.

I put a hand to my cheek, trying to stifle the gasp that wants to rip its way from my throat.

I'm so pathetic. Just pathetic. A girl crying as her cheating fiancée's younger brother calls her to give her a Dear John letter. So cliché.

"Where are you?" Eric asks. His voice is somewhat muffled, like he's on the road or something. *Probably cruising Paris with Phillip and a certain brunette.* Eric's a playboy, so I wouldn't expect anything less from him. Girls throw themselves at Eric all the time.

"What do you want?" I ask tiredly. "Did Phillip put you up to this?"

"What?" he asks, confused. "No."

"Oh, so I'm sure this is just a phone call between friends." I make sure he can hear the sarcasm dripping in my voice.

"Yes, it is, you idiot," he says, and I can hear a hint of amusement in his voice.

"I'm not an idiot," I say thinly, letting my irritation mask the pain. Another emotion other than hurt feels good on me and I want to cling to this like it's my lighthouse in the darkness of despair.

"No. You're not an idiot. Not by a longshot." There's a warmth to him that I didn't expect, and it piques my curiosity even more. "I'm calling to... never mind. Where are you? Right now?"

"I'm at the airport. Why?"

"Thought you'd be. Are you through security yet?"

I frown and glance around. Are there paparazzi heading my way? "Why?"

"Have you bought your ticket yet?"

"Why are you asking me this?"

"Just tell me," he groans. "No, wait, don't. I see you right now. Hang on."

"What?"

But the line is dead.

My mind goes blank as I turn around, and, for a moment, I don't see anything. Then, the automatic doors slide open, revealing Eric looking more flustered than I've ever seen him before. He's not one to get flustered, a necessity since the tabloids and gossip magazines focus on him and his extracurricular affairs.

Well, I guess those tabloids are focusing on Phillip now, too.

Eric's eyes are locked on me, making my stomach twist uncomfortably. There's something so similar yet different about him compared to Phillip. While they are both tall with dark hair and intense blue eyes, their demeanors are night and day. Phillip is always buttoned up, proper to a fault, and always polite and reserved. Loud, cocky, and spoiled, Eric is quite the opposite. I imagine that growing up with the knowledge that you weren't going to have a country resting on your shoulders gave Eric a much more carefree personality than his older brother.

"How did you—? Where did you—?"

The fragments of sentences fall out of my mouth,

because I can honestly say that I've never been this surprised before. I mean, I'm in Venice and the news broke less than two hours ago. What the hell is he doing here? I know that Dubreva is very close to Venice, but he got here eerily fast.

He strides right up to me, and I'm still rooted to the spot. Standing this close, I realize that he's a few inches (or centimeters, we're in Europe after all) taller than his brother. And in his $5,000 Armani suit, he's more imposing than Phillip, for sure.

Except, he's looking down at me and his face falls. "I'm so sorry."

I suck in air through my nose, bristling at his words. "What are you doing here? Did Phillip send you?"

He frowns and shakes his head. "No."

"He did, didn't he?" I say, crossing my arms. "The asshole couldn't tell me himself that he was cheating on me?"

"No, I'm here for *you*," he says. "I haven't talked to my asshole brother, and, frankly, I don't want to, not after the shit he pulled." He sighs and pinches the bridge of his nose.

It's the same gesture that Phillip does when he's annoyed. Despite their differences, the two are like mirrors. With a sinking feeling, I realize that I used to find that endearing when Phillip did it. Many times, it was because I was teasing him and he got frustrated.

Our relationship was like that—we'd have fun with each other.

"You challenge me," Phillip said once when I asked him why he was with me. *"You're not afraid to tell me I'm wrong. You have no idea how few people have done that. And I love you for it."*

Oh my god, I don't know if I'm going to be okay after this.

I don't know where they come from, because I thought I'd cried most of them out, but the tears burst like a fucking dam exploded. The world goes into a watery mess and I reach out and cling to the one thing that's closest to me.

Eric.

I don't care. For now, I just need someone to lean on.

And, to my surprise, Eric puts his arms around me and holds me as I cry right in the middle of the fucking airport.

The perfect end to my bachelorette party.

4
CARA

Even after the tears stop, I count all the prime numbers to 977 in my head before Eric speaks again.

"Where are you headed?" he asks thickly.

His words break me out of my trance, and I straighten up, looking at the departure boards. It's been twenty minutes. Twenty minutes of me bawling my eyes out into the chest of my ex-fiancée's brother. I'm sure someone snapped a picture of that and it will appear all over the news tonight. I may not be that recognizable, but everyone in Europe would recognize Eric Celestro di'Vale.

I glance back at him and his face doesn't betray any annoyance about that. If anything, he looks...*sad*...

Which is...strange.

I cough and cross my arms, putting up a physical barrier between us. His face twitches slightly as he observes my closed posture and I see a mask come down over his features, making his expression unreadable.

"I haven't figured where I'm going yet," I admit truthfully. "I mean, all I have is the American Express Black that Phillip gave me and I don't know if I'm allowed to use it right now or if I'd get arrested for using his credit card, and I don't know if I should go back to Dubreva or stay in Europe or go home or—"

"Don't," he whispers, stopping my ramble. "Don't go back to America."

I gulp down some much-needed air. I'd just been leaning towards that as an option before he showed up. "Don't go back?"

"Yes."

A nervous laugh escapes my throat. "Why not? I'm American after all."

"Yes, but why?"

He seems to be struggling to see my point of view, and I scoff loudly.

"It's home. We don't all have the luxury of flying off to wherever the fuck we feel like." That last part came out too bitter, so I add softly, "Sorry. I guess I'm just so surprised to see you here."

Eric frowns and looks at me. He reaches out and squeezes my shoulder. "Yes, but would running home make you happy?"

Good question. I bite my bottom lip, considering it. No, doing the walk of shame and living with my parents after this debacle would *not* make me happy.

So, what would make me happy then? Not having a cheating fiancée? Never losing sight of my own goals? Crawling into a hole and hiding for seventeen years?

"Where else can I go?" I ask helplessly, shrugging. "I just...want to hide from all of this."

A small grin pulls at his lips, an empathetic one. "If you could go anywhere to hide, where would you go?"

"What?" I laugh uncomfortably.

He shrugs. "It's just a question. You do know that those paparazzi vultures are going to follow you whether you stay in Europe or go back to America. In fact, I'm sure they're at your parents' farm right now."

I hadn't thought of that, and my mouth opens and closes as I try to form an answer.

Instead, all that comes out is, "My parents don't

live on a farm." I'd hardly consider Springfield to be farm country, but I guess it's a world apart from the ancient, densely populated island of Dubreva.

"Regardless..."

He puts another hand on my shoulder and bends down to peer at me, eye-to-eye. I stifle the urge to squirm underneath the intensity of his gaze. This is almost too close for comfort, especially considering recent news.

"If you could choose anywhere in the world to hide," he says again, "where would you go?"

I look at him skeptically, and he presses me again. "Where, Cara?"

"New Zealand."

It pops out of my mouth before I have time to fully process it, and he blinks several times. I can tell that it's the last place he would have expected me to say. Hell, it's the last place *I* expected to say.

I lick my lips and pull away from him, glad to be away from that intense gaze. I shoulder my bag awkwardly and look down at the floor, feeling the blush spread across my cheeks. "My friend Christabel is from there, and while I never visited and she's in London now, I always wanted to go there, and you asked and it was the first place I thought of—"

"Hush," he says, and that single word silences me. I ramble when I'm nervous. "It's perfect. I mean, I never would have thought of it. Which means that no one else would either."

"Well, good," I say, wondering where this conversation is going.

"So," he says, a sly smile curving his lips as he takes out his phone from his pocket. "Let's get going."

"Going where?"

"New Zealand. Like you said."

"*What?* We can't go there." That was meant to be a wish. Nothing more than that.

He shrugs nonchalantly as he takes me by the arm, leading me away from the departures board. "I have my private jet here. So, you'll just arrive there, unexpected, anonymous, and with enough time to figure out what will make you happy."

"You're crazy."

He grins at me. "I'm rich. And my brother hurt you. *Deeply.*" That last part was said like a swear word, and he takes a breath, recovering. "It's the least I can do."

"The least?" I stutter. "Eric, that's...that's..."

He raises an eyebrow as he dials a number on his

phone and raises it to his ear. "Dashing? Generous? Gallant?"

"*Kidnapping.*" It's not really, but he's leading me away without my full permission to a point on the very opposite end of the world.

He gives me an unimpressed look as someone on the other line answers. "Herbert?" he says, and I recognize the name of his valet. "Prep the G650. And I hope you're ready to be my co-pilot on a long-haul flight." He looks at me slyly. "Come on, Cara," he says to me. "A bit of an escape before you have to go back to stark reality."

I don't know what it is, whether it's his exuberance that feels like sunshine on my broken heart or the thought of not having to face the consequences of Phillip's infidelity, but I nod.

"Okay. Sure. Why the hell not?"

5

ERIC

This is literally the worst idea I've ever had. And I've had plenty of those in my time.

I don't know what came over me. I arrived at the airport, and at first, I was relieved to see that she hadn't run from my life, not yet.

I was going to tell her everything.

And then she started crying and I realized how heartbroken she is. I can't tell her. I can't add to this, not now. She's not last year's Ferrari that has been cast aside for a newer model. She's a woman with her own hopes and dreams, which have now been shattered.

She really does love Phillip.

I couldn't put her through that.

So, then I come up with this harebrained

scheme. And I 100% agree with Cara when she said that I'm crazy.

Herbert is giving me the death-glare as I prep the plane for departure. The death-glare isn't so much an angry glare as it is one of disappointment, which is probably worse.

I try to ignore him, but I've spent twenty-seven years underneath that glare. Herbert first gave it to me when I was caught in a lie after stealing Phillip's shoes when we were toddlers. And he's done it all the countless times that I've woken up next to a toilet after a night of drinking.

It never gets any easier. Herbert's had a lot of practice with the death-glare.

Finally, the tension in me snaps.

"What?" I ask like a spoiled child. I don't look at him as I say it.

"What are you doing?"

"I'm preparing to fly to Singapore." And then Singapore to Queenstown. When Cara randomly chose New Zealand as her getaway, she certainly did pick the other side of the world. It caught me off-guard, but if anything, it reinforces just how much she wants to get away from this shitstorm.

I feel for her. I really do. It doesn't help that I'm in love with her, too.

"That's not what I mean," Herbert sighs. "You're going to end up hurting her worse. This foolish trip. The manipulation."

I grit my teeth. "There's no manipulation."

Herbert raises an eyebrow, increasing the intensity of his death-glare enough to make me squirm. "So, am I to believe that you're just taking Miss Van Meter to a different country all out of the goodness of your heart? That you're not planning on seducing her or otherwise have intentions that are not impure?"

"That's right." Because I'm not going to betray her trust. I'm not going to do anything that she doesn't want to do...

"Eric..." he starts.

"Everything all right?"

We both turn around in our seat to see Cara standing in the doorway to the cockpit.

"Yep," I say, masking my embarrassment with a cocky grin. It's a skill I've mastered throughout my whole life. "We're just prepping for takeoff. Did you message your friends and family that you're going on a trip to get away from everything?"

It won't do to have a manhunt for her while she disappears.

She nods absently. "Yep. Although I'm not sure how long that excuse will work."

"It's the truth."

"Yes, it is. You know," she says softly, indicating the cockpit. "I don't think I'll ever get used to flying private jets." Then she chuckles at herself and twirls a strand of hair between her thumb and index finger. "I guess, after this, I won't get to, will I?"

"You have an open invitation any time you'd like," I tell her truthfully. Herbert's death-glare hardens a centimeter more, and I force my discomfort aside as I focus on her.

"Thanks," she says. "But I don't think you'll come out to Missouri very much after this."

I want to tell her that isn't true. But then again, I don't know what will happen to her when we're done with our little escape. I don't want to lie to her. She's had enough of that in the past few hours. Or however long Phillip's been cheating on her.

Our eyes connect for the briefest moment, and I see the innocence that has been badly damaged. Her innocence has always been refreshing after so many people trying to take advantage of me and my position my entire life.

No wonder Phillip was drawn to her. No wonder I'm so pissed off for her sake.

What an asshole. And when I think that, I don't know if I'm referring to him or myself.

I clear my throat, realizing that in my assessment of Cara, there's been an awkward, long pause between the three of us. I can tell that even though he looks as calm and collected as ever, Herbert is pissed because he usually smooths over any moments like this.

"Are you going to be all right back there?" I ask Cara. "Without a flight crew and everything?"

I could have hired a crew here, but given the nature of this particular flight and how quickly it was arranged, I didn't want to spend time finding people to serve Cara.

She shakes her head. "Honestly? No, I won't be." She points with her thumb towards the tail of the plane. "But I'll be glad for the peace and quiet. It'll give me time to think." A pained look comes over her face and her eyes start glistening.

"Oh, speaking of," I say, holding out my hand. "Give me your phone."

She frowns. I can almost see the alarm bells going off in her head. "Why?"

"If this is an escape, you need to stay off your phone. Turn off the location, turn the whole bloody thing off. Otherwise, after a few days, you're going to have the entire country of Dubreva knocking on your door." I smirk, meaning to encourage her. "Trust me, there are plenty of times when I've had to go off the grid because I was doing something I shouldn't. There are going to be points where you'll want to see what people are saying. And you're going to regret it."

Our eyes meet, the doubt in hers clashing against mine, but I stand my ground. "Okay," she says. "Okay."

She pulls it out of the back of her jeans pocket and hands it to me. I swipe to the home screen and switch the tracking off—as I said, I've done this plenty of times before, so I know what I'm doing. I turn it off, knowing that should be it.

Then, the *pièce de résistance*: I hand the phone over to Herbert, who raises an eyebrow. Cara blubbers a protest.

"Oh," she says. Her bottom lip quivers, and she bites it to stop. She brings up her right hand and takes off the enormous engagement ring Phillip gave her. It was our grandmother's, and it has been in the family for generations. She lets out a deep breath and hands the ring to Herbert. "Can you hold onto this?" she asks. "It's not really mine anymore. Just... don't lose it."

Herbert nods, almost approvingly. "I will guard this with my life, Miss Van Meter."

She nods, the spark of tears filling her eyes.

"Listen," I say, placating her. "This is meant to be an escape. Away from everything. And everything will be all right." I push her even further, hating myself for it. "Do you trust me?"

Even though I'm taking her to some far-off place, hoping to have a bit more time with her, to help her forget everything. And, possibly, hoping that she'll fall in love with me. Like I am with her.

God, I'm a fucking manipulative prick. I hate myself in this moment.

She narrows her eyes at me, and at first, I think she's going to say that no, she doesn't trust me—in which case, I'd be devastated. But she smiles and nods.

"You're right, I need an escape," she says vaguely. "Besides, I've got a few books on my Kindle that I need to catch up on."

"Turn off the wi-fi. Reporters are without scruples."

She gave me a thumbs-up and one of her trademark goofy smiles. I am in for some serious trouble.

"You're sure you'll be okay back there by yourself?" Maybe leaving her mostly alone for 48 hours may not be the best idea. I make a mental note to check up on her as much as I can. When I'm not flying the plane, that is.

"Yeah, I don't need a flight crew. Besides, I never got used to being waited on hand and foot. No offence, Herbert," she adds quickly.

"None taken," he adds blithely. "I think of myself as more of the voice of reason for His Majesty. He doesn't listen to me as much as I'd like, though."

I could kill him right now. But Cara laughs and places a strand of hair behind her ear. I have to still my own hand from doing it for her as I watch, fascinated. "All right, then, I'll leave you guys to your job." She bites her bottom lip in such a sexy way, enough that my cock hardens in response. "Eric?"

"Yeah?"

"Thanks." She sighs. "It's crazy to go to New Zealand right now, but..." Her voice trails off and she looks at me again. "Maybe crazy is what I need. So, thank you."

"No worries," I say in a horrible imitation of a Kiwi accent. Dubrevian was my first language, and that accent permeates every word I speak, including English. It makes Kiwi accents hard to mimic.

Cara only smiles in response before heading back to the cabin and closing the door.

I let out a long breath as I resituate myself in my seat. "Still think it's a bad idea, Herbert?"

He purses his lips. "Do you want the truth, your Majesty, or the fake validation that you seek?"

"I see you still haven't come around to the idea yet." I put my headset on so I don't have to hear any more of his bitching. But Herbert still gets in the last word, with an uncharacteristically harsh phrase that tells me just how little he approves of this.

"I don't have enough NDA forms for all of this bullshit."

6

CARA

The first thing I notice when I step off the plane in Queenstown is the blast of cold air.

"Holy shit!"

I am eloquent about it, too.

It was summertime when we left Venice. Here, it's the dead of winter. And while I had mentally been prepared for it, it still floors me. I only have summer clothes in my bags. I figured that I could buy a jacket and just wash my one pair of jeans every day, but I realize now that it won't be enough.

Herbert smirks at me as he helps me down the stairs. The cold doesn't appear to bother him one bit as he takes my hand in his gloved one and helps me take my first step onto New Zealand soil. He doesn't look the worse for wear even though I feel like I've been battered and strung out over the last few days.

Oh yeah, I've been crying a lot. That's why. I probably look like death warmed over, but the valet doesn't say anything regarding my appearance.

I'm grateful for that.

Now that I've got my bearings, I take stock of the world around me. I'm on the frozen airstrip with a glittering town in the distance, bordered by snow-capped mountains and a lake. It feels like I've stepped into a storybook frozen in time. Like this is a moment that epics are made of.

I'm in New Zealand. Two days ago, I was in Venice with my bachelorette party, and then I found out about—

I shut my eyes, blocking both the beautiful town around me and the horrible thoughts edging their way into my mind. When I wasn't failing at trying to read or binge Netflix on the plane, I was curled up into a ball and sobbing over my failed relationship. A few times, Eric and Herbert came back to the cabin to check up on me. I'm sure they saw the tears, because the check-ups were more infrequent after that.

2…3…5…7…11…13…

A hand falls on my shoulder, making me jump. I

blink up at Eric who is giving me a lopsided smile. "We're here," he says. "Finally. Is it everything you ever wanted?"

I look back at the plane. "Don't you have to...park it? Or something?" Phillip has a private jet that I've been on, but he doesn't fly it, so it never occurred to me what happens to them when they land.

Much like it never occurred to me to worry about Phillip when I'm not around him.

Stop it, Cara. I suck in a deep breath, forcing back the tears that threaten to fall. I've been torturing myself with this kind of thinking for two days now.

Eric follows my gaze back at the jet and shrugs. "Herbert will take care of that."

The valet's smirk falls and I see his eyes harden just a smidge towards Eric. He nods stiffly as he goes back up the stairs.

"Is he okay?" I ask.

Eric nods. "He'll be fine. He's just cranky after flying so much in the past few days."

I cross my arms. "Kind of lucky that your valet is also a pilot."

"He's the reason why I'm a pilot and joined the Dubrevian Air Force." I curiously raise an eyebrow. "He taught me how to fly," Eric adds.

"That's amazing. You two must spend a lot of

time together." Phillip always had a few different valets, none that were as close to him as I can tell Eric and Herbert are.

Eric combs a hand through his hair. "Yeah, well, the man practically raised me."

I look back at the prince. It's so weird looking at him, because he looks so much like Phillip, yet their facial expressions are so different.

Stop thinking about Phillip. This is supposed to be an escape from all that.

"You must have been a real handful," I say as we start walking towards the terminal.

He chuckles. "Still am."

I GAPE out of the limo window as we curve our way around the mountains towards the city of Queenstown. Snowcapped mountains surround us, and Lake Wakatipu borders one side of it, reflecting the early morning light. While I've been to Switzerland and the Alps, there is a rawness to this landscape. I get the feeling that there are so many places here that haven't been seen by human eyes.

It's absolutely breathtaking, to the point where I literally have to remember to breathe.

Entry into the country is easy. No one recognized me as the bride-to-be of the crown prince of Dubreva. And if they recognized Eric based on his passport, they didn't say anything. Rather, the immigration official stamped our passports and said in a Kiwi accent that I'm still getting acclimated to, "Welcome to New Zillund."

Anonymity. That's exactly what I want here.

We're driving on the left side of the road, which feels unfamiliar to me as we wind our way to the city center. The roads are narrow and hug the side of the lake, almost overwhelming in how close we are to going over the side. At one point, it's too much and I sigh and sit back in my seat.

2...3...5...7...11...

Eric quirks an eyebrow at me.

"You okay?"

I wring my hands. I don't know why exactly. My stomach is just twisting with nervous energy at being on the other side of the world when Phillip—my *ex*-fiancée is probably wondering where I am.

Good.

Still, though, I wring.

"I just can't believe we're here," I say finally.

He gives me a smug smile. "That's what happens

when you have a private jet. You can go to the other side of the world anytime you wish."

"You're the one with the private jet."

He chuckles. "Yes, I am."

"Why?" The question pops out of my mouth before I fully think about it, but when it does, I realize how valid it is. Why would Phillip's brother be interested in taking me to New Zealand? Why would he even care?

His eyes burn into mine for a second before he chuckles and lowers the privacy screen between us and the driver's seat. Herbert is driving the limo. Apparently, the man can drive anything with pedals.

"Your Majesty?" Herbert says evenly.

"We should probably stop downtown so the lady can get some more, ah, seasonal clothing." He looks back at me, giving me an appraising look. "She looks miserable."

"Well, you say what's on your mind," I say, offended by his description of me. I don't tell him that it's true. I can't stop shivering.

"One thing you need to know about me, Cara," Eric says as he shifts to fish something out of his back pocket. "I will always tell you the truth if you ask. And I'll make sure that you're dressed for the weather. Here, you can go shopping on me."

He pulls out his American Express Black and offers it to me. I look at it and freeze.

The similarity between this gesture and Phillip's American Express Black in my own purse isn't lost on me.

"I'm fine," I say, crossing my arms. I'm gritting my teeth. "I don't need that."

He blinks in surprise. "What?"

"I don't need your money," I say. "I'll be fine."

"Cara—"

"I'm not some charity case for you, Eric," I retort, refusing to look at him. Then again, he's flown me halfway across the world to get away from my own demons. He could get a fucking tax break off that amount of charity.

Suddenly, that impulsive decision makes me feel sick.

"You're not a charity case," he says.

"I certainly feel like one," I mutter.

The pause between us extends uncomfortably, and the card wavers. Finally, Eric pockets the black credit card without another comment.

I sigh in relief. With Phillip, that would have been an argument. He's always been more buttoned up than his younger brother, and, in his view, he always takes care of me. Eric is...different.

And once again, I'm comparing the two brothers. I need to stop that.

"Thank you," I whisper. "That means a lot."

He gives me a hard look. "The offer stands if at any point you change your mind. But I know when I'm losing a battle."

"No you don't," Herbert retorts from the driver's seat.

Eric twists around and glares at him, and I laugh softly. He blinks and looks back at me, as if there's a joke he's not getting.

"All right," Eric says, "but let Herbert stay with you. He can carry your bags or give you a credit card if you change your mind. I'll, uh, go make sure that the rental house is up to snuff."

"His Majesty, driving himself," Herbert mutters from the front seat. "I'm shocked."

I think I'm starting to like the older man.

"Thank you," I say sincerely. "For all this. I just... want to do something by myself for a change."

I'd been with Phillip for four years now, and I'm just now realizing that I lost a part of who I was during that time. I'm Cara Van Meter. I wanted to be a math professor at a university once. Not a princess.

I learned too late that fairy tales don't come true.

But, dammit, I'm going to work to find my own story again. Even if that is with my old credit card.

Eric glances back at me, a hundred different emotions playing across his face. Some of them I think I recognize, but I don't understand why they're there.

I feel the inertia of the car stop, and Eric gestures to the window, his expression falling into a cocky, lopsided smile again as he starts to move to the door. "We're here."

Two hundred and ninety-eight dollars.

The winter coat in the storefront, rated for the deep of winter, is nearly three hundred New Zealand dollars. Based on the money conversion kiosks at the airport, I quickly do the math in my head to convert it to US dollars, my default for any sort of money conversion. Sure, I'd been living in Europe and used the British Pound Sterling at Oxford, and then the Euro when I lived in Dubreva, but there's something comforting about switching back to your old currency, especially when mental math comes easily to you.

$210.75 in US dollars. Give or take a few tenths of a cent.

My stomach drops at how big of a chunk that will take out of my available credit. Compounded by the fact that I have no idea how long we're going to stay here, if I'm going to make the money stretch, I'm going to have to be wiser with it.

It's amazing how just last week, I wouldn't even blink at a price tag like that.

Ugh, what happened to me? I disgust myself with that kind of thinking.

"Miss Van Meter?" Herbert asks behind me. "Are you going in?"

"Uhm," I say, glancing back at him. He doesn't look impatient or bored, just accommodating. I wonder what he thinks of this entire thing, but nothing betrays his thoughts. I guess he's used to it, being Eric's valet.

I step back, looking at the store's name. Kiwi Souvenirs. Not the most original name, and it tells me that I'm at a very touristy stop. But curiosity gets the better of me. When in Rome, right? And since my last trip to Italy was such a disaster, I think I'll be going the tourist route this time.

"Yes, I'm going in," I tell the valet.

I step inside, welcoming the warmth inside the store. Herbert quietly follows me.

I guess it's my pride, but I want to prove that I can pay for things myself.

Granted, you didn't pay for the flight down here.

Extenuating circumstances, but I still feel guilty about it and I probably owe Eric some sort of big thanks for helping me. The worst part is, I probably can't ever him pay back for all this.

You know his reputation. He'd probably gladly let you pay him back in a physical way.

I *do* know his reputation. But that doesn't make it right. And I'm not that kind of girl, even if he is that kind of guy. Even if we are on some sort of crazy escape to the bottom of the world.

But it could be a great way to get back at Phillip.

No. I won't do it. Refuse to. We're here platonically. For all I know, Eric wanted to get out of Europe as much as I wanted to get off this planet.

A mental image pops into my head. Of the two of us locked in a 69 position, his rock-hard naked body over mine, showing me all that he can do, considering all the practice he's had in his time.

Before I know it, my cheeks are red, and I'm counting prime numbers without realizing.

"Miss Van Meter?" Herbert prompts again.

"I'm sorry, I just got distracted," I tell him, embarrassed.

I make the decision that I'm better than "thanking" Eric that way. This is strictly between friends. That's it.

I'll have to show him my gratitude in a different way. Like cooking him dinner.

That sparks up an idea. I used to work at a French restaurant. Maybe I can do prepare him a nice, fancy meal. Granted, I was never good in the kitchen, but it's the thought that counts, right?

Right.

The store is quaint. A few plush kiwi birds, some boots and rugs made of sheepskin, and some abalone plates, along with all the usual trappings of "I Heart NZ" sweatshirts.

As I peruse the shop, my hand falls on a black zip-up fleece-lined jacket with the island country screen-printed in pink on the back. I glance at the price tag, and sigh in relief.

$38.10. It's still expensive for a sweater, but what did I expect from a souvenir shop off Queenstown's main strip?

"Does the rental have a washing machine?" I ask Herbert.

He blinks and nods. "Indeed. I imagine you're planning on using it?"

"Probably," I say, picking out my size. I imagine I'll be wearing this hoodie a lot.

The valet raises an eyebrow at my choice in clothing. Then, ever so slightly, his lips pull up in a smile. It's probably the least sexy thing ever, and I'm sure it's nothing like he'd ever expect a prince's ex-fiancée to wear. It's a smile of approval.

Yep, I'm liking Herbert now.

I grab an accompanying "I Heart NZ" sweater, this one a bit cheaper than the zip-up hoodie. Between the two layers, I'll have a decent way of keeping myself warm. Otherwise, I'll be wearing blankets around the rental.

I walk over towards the register and the cashier smiles at me. "*Kia ora,*" she greets warmly. "Find everything all right?"

"I did," I say.

"First time in Queenstown?"

"First time in New Zealand."

"Well," the cashier says, eying my jacket and my thin shirt, "welcome to winter."

"Yeah," I laugh uneasily. I must look like an idiot, because it's below freezing outside and I'm barely dressed for anything colder than a summer day.

With that thought, I toss some knitted mittens on the counter that are on a shelf next to it. A well-placed impulse buy if I've ever seen one. I also notice a rack of discounted beanies and grab one of those, too.

I hold my breath and count my prime numbers as the cashier rings up everything and nearly sigh in relief when it all comes out to $119.90 in New Zealand dollars, or a little less than $87 in US dollars. Much cheaper than the coat I saw in the window.

And, I guess if I look like a ridiculous tourist, that issue of "thanking" Eric won't ever come up. He'd never be interested in someone decked out in all New Zealand apparel. The thought is almost comforting, although there's a weird heat in my cheeks that I can't shake.

I hand over my own credit card to the cashier, deducting the total from my line of credit. Being a math whiz, I'll memorize the bill and obsess over how to pay for it. 18.9% APR over three months is…

Stop, Cara. You're freaking yourself out.

I can easily go down a rabbit hole thinking about the numbers, so I blink furiously and look away as the cashier inserts my card into the machine. Then I see it.

What the...?

I pick it up and nearly drop it as an embarrassed giggle escapes my throat.

"A possum fur willy warmer?" I read, asking the cashier to make sure that my eyes aren't playing a trick on me. It's a...cock ring?...made out of a fluffy brown, almost feathery fur. At least I think it is.

They sell that kind of stuff in a souvenir shop here? I've seen sexual gag stuff before in tourist traps —in fact, the other day, I was laughing at penis-shaped pasta in Venice—but this is a little overt.

The cashier responds with a wry smile. "100 per cent New Zealand possum fur. Very popular with the guys, I reckon."

I can't imagine Phillip ever wearing one of those. Now, Eric...*maybe...*

Again, I feel the heat between my legs as I imagine the prince naked, his rock-hard abs leading down to the willy warmer around his dick. It's no longer funny...it feels like I'm doing something that I shouldn't.

For the second time in five minutes. What's wrong with me?

I take a deep breath and hastily put it back. I see the flicker of disappointment in the cashier's face, but she turns back and starts bagging everything up.

"Oh, I'll just wear that out," I say, grabbing my purchases and tearing the tags off. I put the sweater over my clothes and zip the hoodie over everything and shove my hands and head into the mittens and beanie.

Yep, I feel less sexy now. The heat I felt disappears like the New Zealand wind whipped away the warmth from inside the store.

Herbert has a small smile as I walk past him. "I can tell you're getting into the kiwi spirit, Miss Van Meter," he says mildly.

"Please, call me Cara," I tell him as I fidget and tuck a sleeve underneath a mitten. "I'm no royal. Also, I didn't go anywhere near as crazy as I could have in there."

His eyes flick back to the counter where the rack of willy warmers is waiting and the smile grows, just a tad more. "You're right," he says. "My sincerest apologies."

I laugh as we start walking, then I remember my thought about repaying Eric back by cooking him dinner. I remember seeing a store that looked something like a supermarket.

"Hey Herbert," I say, catching the old man's attention. "Do you think we have time to go grocery shopping?"

7
ERIC

By any definition, I'm a spoiled prick, so I literally have no idea how this rental house—*bach*, as Kiwis call it—stacks up in the eyes of someone who grew up on a farm (no, Cara didn't grow up on a farm, she says, I have to remember that).

But I admit, even to me, it feels swank.

It's a three-bedroom modern house, but every room is cavernous with a stone fireplace and king-size bed with 1500 thread count sheets and plush carpets. There's a large kitchen and a great room that more resembles a lodge than a home. An outdoor deck has a fire pit and a barbecue, along with ample seating for entertaining.

It's luxury at its finest.

I stand in one of the bedrooms, looking out the floor-to-ceiling windows that overlook the lake bordering the town. The impossibly blue water reflects the brilliant sky, and the town sits in a cold, winter slumber, surrounded by mountains. There's something so peaceful, so quaint about it.

Cara couldn't have chosen a better place to escape reality.

And it's the perfect place to get closer to her.

I block the thought out of my head. No, I've brought her here as a friend. If anything, else happens, it will be on her terms. It will be because she wants it, not because I want it. Hell, after getting everything that I've ever wanted, being denied should be refreshing.

It really fucking isn't.

I glance behind me at the room. It's the smallest room, but it's in the most secluded part of the house and there are feminine touches to the bedspread that the other rooms don't have. I imagine this will be the room where Cara sleeps. I should probably take the one on the far opposite end. Not that I'd try anything, but I don't want to tempt fate.

I check my Rolex for the time. The time difference between New Zealand and Dubreva is starting to hit me and I'm exhausted, especially after flying long-haul like that. Herbert is supposed to call me when they're done so I can take the limo and pick them up. It shouldn't be too much longer. I get the feeling that her finances won't keep her shopping for hours. I wonder if she'll ask Herbert to borrow my card.

A part of me hopes she doesn't change her mind. I *like* that she has that kind of fire. I caught that stubborn gleam in her eye in the car.

I pinch the bridge of my nose and sigh heavily.

You're doing this for her. Not for you. Right. Be the better man, Eric. For once.

I take a deep sigh and turn back to the lake, and movement catches my eye. Cara and Herbert are walking up the path to the house. Walking when I said that I could pick them up.

Between the two of them, they're carrying plastic shopping bags, although I can't see what they are. They're talking, too. And, for the first time since this whole trip started, Cara is smiling genuinely and unabashedly.

To my utter surprise.

I storm out of the bedroom, throwing on my blazer as I exit the house and jog down the path to meet them.

"Greetings, your Majesty," Herbert says, pursing

his lips. He knows I'm unhappy with him and I'm glaring at him.

"Hey, I thought I was picking you up," I say, wincing inwardly at how possessive I sound. It's not that I am—it's that I didn't want Cara having to do any work. "And what's all this?" I take both bags from Cara.

"Groceries," she says as I realize what they are. "For dinner tonight."

"Dinner?" I ask. "But I made reservations at this place—"

"*I'm* cooking tonight," Cara says, taking the bags back from me. "It's the least I can do."

I blink. "For what?"

"For bringing me here," she says slyly as she brushes past me. "I worked at a restaurant when I studied at Oxford, remember?"

"Oh, I remember all right," I tell her. "My lap is still sore from that soup."

She averts her eyes and looks down ashamedly. Maybe now wasn't the right time to bring that up.

I glance back at Herbert, who shrugs nonchalantly. "She insisted, sir."

The old man likes seeing me squirm. Cara catches on too, and takes a few steps backwards to give a hearty laugh. It's at my expense, but it's good to see anything on her other than despair.

Then I notice what she's wearing. She looks like an advertisement for Kiwi souvenirs.

"*That's* what you got for winter?" I should have insisted she go shopping with my credit card.

The laughter dies and she frowns. "It's good enough," she says with a shrug. "Is that the rental?" She nods up the hill to the house.

I lick my lips, sensing the walls she's putting up around her heart again. "It is."

She nods. "Cool beans." She turns away and briskly walks away, widening the gap between us. I'm left with Herbert at the back.

"I like her, sir," my valet says under his breath.

I look down at him in surprise. "You *like* her?" I don't think he's said anything similar to that in all the time that I've known him. He's seen me bring so many girls back to my bed, and never once has he indicated that he liked any of them.

Granted, you're not bringing Cara to your bed, but...

"Indeed I do," the old man says. "She's different. Pure. Independent." He gives me a hard look. "Keeps you on your toes."

I comb a hand through my hair. "That she does."

Herbert shifts the bags of groceries to one hand,

and then puts his other hand on my shoulder and gives it a squeeze. At first, I think he's going to say something encouraging. His blessing of this whole harebrained thing. But then he says, "Don't you fucking dare go breaking her heart, sir."

I guess I deserve that.

WE END up having to order pizza delivery anyway.

"You used to work at a restaurant, you say?" I tease before I pick up another slice of pizza.

Despite the disaster that was Cara's attempt at a *Blanquette de Veau*, this pizza is, in short, *amazing*. I knew that New Zealand exported a lot of their cheese to Europe—I just never realized how good their dairy truly is.

Even in the flickering light of the fire in the fire pit, I can see the blush creeping in on Cara's face.

"Apparently, it's not just like riding a bicycle," she says. "French cooking, that is. Although I still blame the stove." The stove that caught fire and ruined her dish.

"I think you, me, and French food don't get along," I say.

She nods in agreement.

We're sitting out on the deck while the kitchen airs out. The night air is crisp, turning our breaths into puffs of white. Cara is bundled up in her touristy garb, and while she's huddled under a blanket, she doesn't seem to be uncomfortably cold.

She picks up her third slice of pizza, and I can't help but marvel that this is a woman who has no pretenses about who she is or her image. She is comfortable in her own skin, and isn't worried about a few extra calories from another slice of pizza.

"You did better than me," I say candidly. "I wouldn't even know how to turn on the stove."

She chuckles softly. "Yeah, I'm not a great cook. Give me advanced calculus and I can solve that for you in a microsecond. But cooking? Terrible. But not as terrible as Phillip. I tried teaching him how to make macaroni and cheese—you know, the kind out of the boxes?"

"With the radioactive orange cheese powder?"

She laughs, a full-bellied laugh now. "Yeah. Anyways, I tried teaching him. Left him alone for one minute. *One minute.* And he dumped the cheese packet in. Didn't even drain the pasta."

At my blank look, she continues laughing, harder.

"You're supposed to drain the pasta, sir," Herbert

says, setting down a glass of New Zealand sauvignon blanc in front of both us before heading back to the house. At least the wine survived the cooking disaster.

"I gathered that," I say grumpily, picking up my glass.

Cara leans forward, the firelight reflecting in her eyes as she looks off at a point somewhere in the mountains, and she sighs heavily. "I had some good times with Phillip," she admits quietly. "Good times that...are irrelevant now."

I take a sip, waiting for her to continue. She simply watches the fire, her face unreadable, although I can imagine she's hurting deep inside.

Finally, she speaks, her voice soft, broken. "Why did he do it, Eric?"

I consider my answer for a long time before speaking. How do you even answer a question like that? From the woman you love about the brother she loves?

"He's used to not being left wanting for anything," I tell her. "When we were kids, we'd just cry and fifteen different people would jump to do anything to make us stop. And, when we got older, that kind of thinking just stuck. Phillip must have seen something he wanted and..." My voice trails off, because I'm hearing too much of myself in my words.

"Is that the way you are?"

She's looking at me now, wide-eyed and vulnerable. I close my eyes, blocking those sad eyes out.

"Yes," I admit truthfully.

There's a long pause between us, and I want to take back my words. Then again, I asked her for her trust, and I'm not about to break that, no matter how bad it makes me out to be. I'm used to getting everything I want.

And I want to be honest with her.

Even if that ends up pushing her away from me.

"Thank you for telling me the truth," she whispers, confirming that I did the right thing, even though it's ripping me apart from the inside out.

I nod slowly.

I find myself watching her bottom lip, wanting her to bite it. Or, better yet, have *me* bite it.

I could take her right now out here, make her forget that she ever cared about Phillip.

No, I can't do that. Not to her.

I sigh and sit back, breaking the spell between us.

She gathers up her blanket and her wine glass. As she moves to get the plates, I put my hand over hers to stop her. She jumps at the touch like it was a live wire and lets out a shuddering breath.

"Leave it, Herbert can get it," I tell her gently.

"I've got this," she says. "I just need to be in control of something right now. That was supposed to be dinner, but…" She snickers. "I can't screw up doing the dishes, right??"

As she goes back into the house, I want to tell her that Phillip cheating on her wasn't her fault. But the door closes behind her.

And I'm left alone in the night.

8
ERIC

There are a lot of sheep in New Zealand, but I'm not able to count any tonight. I'd like to blame my inability to sleep on the time difference, but I know that's not the case.

I lay awake in bed, staring up at the ceiling. Now that the hectic punishment of travel is over, I'm able to lay here and realize just how close Cara is in the house. The thought of her sleeping not too far from me is almost too much to bear.

She may be on the opposite side of the house, but she could be in the same room as me, for how my thoughts are consumed with her.

Is she asleep? Or is she lying in bed too, thinking of Phillip?

And, meanwhile, is my asshole of a brother feeling any remorse for what he's done?

"Fuck," I say, pressing my palms to my eyes. "Fucking hell."

All this pent-up frustration because I saw her first. No, I *fell* for her first, too. She just met Phillip before I could sweep her off her feet.

And if things had been the other way around? Well, I certainly would have never cheated on her. Maybe we'd still be here in New Zealand, on a holiday or a honeymoon. But I'd keep her close and cherish every second of spending my life with her.

I remember the first time I saw her at *Le Petit Cochon*, the French restaurant she worked at in Oxford. She knew her way around French cuisine much better back then.

I was twenty-two, on leave from the Dubreva's Air Force, and in Oxford visiting Phillip who was studying there. He went to university while I enlisted, like a good little citizen. Granted, I already knew how to fly airplanes, so that played a huge part in my decision, but I think it was largely to defy my mother who wanted me to enroll in political science and get some sort of degree.

I know it was.

I was young, stupid, looking for my next lay, and

had zero expectations when I walked into *Le Petit Cochon*. I don't know why, out of all the restaurants in Oxford, I decided to go to that one. Surely a bar would have been better for my mission. But, for some inexplicable reason, I ended up there. I'd sent Herbert back to the hotel, because there's nothing like picking up a chick with an old man hovering behind your back. I had a very low success rate with that method.

I remember sitting down at the table, clasping my hands, and eyeing the restaurant for anyone interesting. I wore sunglasses and it was a chilly night, so I wore my leather jacket. It also served to hide my face slightly.

Even despite the semi-disguise, people noticed me, were talking about me. I'm a prince after all, and having any royalty there was like having the mother fucking Windsors sitting at the table.

Then, my lap met a bowl of *soupe a l'oignon*, and I jolted with a shocked yell of pain, about ready to throw whoever dropped a bowl of hot soup on me.

"WHAT THE FUCK!"

"Holy shit! I'm so sorry!" The voice was American, the strong "r" of her "sorry" giving her away. I looked down to see...*her*.

Her curly red hair, her panicked green eyes.

Freckles on her face. Glasses There was something unconventionally beautiful about her, even though I couldn't put my finger on it. She was scholarly, almost nerdy in her appearance, like she never gave it much thought. Yet, she was comfortable in her own skin without realizing how sexy that was.

It drew me to her.

Being in front of the media my entire life, I know that I've been labeled a heartthrob, an eligible bachelor. I know that there were women who claimed to love me even though they never met me. I never believed in love at first sight.

Until that moment. With my pants soaked with French onion soup, my skin burning, and steaming liquid way too close to my cock for comfort, I believed in love at first sight.

What the hell kind of guy didn't care that he'd nearly been sexually disabled?

"Oh my god," she was exclaiming. "Oh my god, oh my god! I'm so fucking clumsy! I am *so* sorry!" She had no idea who I was, didn't look at me with any recognition. Whether it was the sunglasses or the fact that she had never heard of Dubreva, she had no idea who I was, and I felt that, for the first time ever, I could start with a blank slate with her.

It's a feeling that I'm not used to having.

She grabbed a wet, dirty rag from a nearby table that was being cleaned and started scrubbing at my pants, and I hissed in pain—so, I really was injured. Not only that, she was achingly close to my cock.

I put my hand over hers to stop her scrubbing. She looked up at me with those wide, frightened eyes—I think she knew I was someone famous even at that point—and I offered her a weak smile.

"Don't do that," I panted, half from pain, half from something else. "Just...call an ambulance..."

Our eyes remained connected for a moment longer.

She nodded and with shaky hands, took out her mobile and called the number. I leaned back in my chair and pinched the bridge of my nose to take my mind off the pain in my upper thigh and the weird swirl of emotions running through me.

That had never happened to me before.

By that point, we had drawn the attention of everyone in the restaurant, and an elderly French man stormed over to talk to me. I quickly found out that he was the waitress's boss and that he'd personally escort me to Accident Emergency as a part of his deepest apologies. He was angry with the girl. He was angry with the situation.

Understandably so. A royal just had scalding hot

soup dumped on his leg at his restaurant. Not good for business.

The girl that had been waiting on me looked like she was in deep concentration, her lips moving as she counted or something to keep calm. To her credit, she didn't cry or freak out. She did exactly as her boss told her to do, cleaned up my table and helped me to the ambulance.

As I was being driven to the hospital, I realized, that in the pandemonium, I never even caught her name. I sure got her boss's name, along with a few business cards and gift vouchers to eat for free at the restaurant, but never the waitress's name.

Fortunately, the burns weren't severe (my manhood came out unscathed, thank you, whoever is upstairs). The doctor patched me up and said that it would blister, but otherwise, there wouldn't be scarring.

I spent a night at the hospital. One night. Phillip came to visit me. Herbert stayed with me

And then I went back to the *Le Petit Cochon* to find the girl. She'd been fired. Her boss was worried when I asked for her name, which was ridiculous. Herbert and I had to fight to keep the incident out of the media, rather than put it *into* the media. As the old man likes to complain, he had a lot of NDAs to sign in those few days.

I only got a first name for my waitress, and that was because she was being paid under the table as her visa didn't allow her to work.

But I had a name. *Cara.* And I couldn't find her anywhere, no matter how hard Herbert and I searched.

My leave ended. With my leg mostly healed, I had to go back to the Dubreva Air Force. I didn't tell Phillip about her. We were never close, and he wouldn't understand something like love at first sight. Phillip, the fairy tale prince who didn't believe in fairy tales.

I did now. Except I didn't have anything to go on, no glass slipper to track her down.

A few months later, I got the shock of my life. At Christmas, like some sort of present gone wrong.

Phillip brought a girlfriend back with him to Dubreva for Christmas. Imagine my surprise when the butler opened the front door to the palace and there stood Phillip and *Cara*, there to stay for the holidays.

Out of all the women in Oxford, he had to start dating the one that I was in love with.

She recognized me right away and I saw the

panic on her face. That first day was awkward, she wouldn't meet my eyes and avoided me at all cost. It wasn't until we were all outside in the estate gardens, sipping champagne, that Phillip ran back to the palace for something and I had a chance to be alone with her (or, as alone as a royal in his home can be).

I noticed that she was trying to watch me without looking suspicious. She was scared shitless that I was going to do something. I wanted to, but not want she was thinking.

"So you recognize me now, huh?" I asked, trying to be as nonchalant as possible.

She bit her bottom lip and didn't say anything for a few long heartbeats. "Yes," she admitted. "I mean, I googled Dubreva after Phillip and I started dating, and while there were pictures of you, I just never put it together."

"Never put it together that I was the same guy whose crotch you maimed with French onion soup?"

The color drained from her face, and I immediately regretted bringing it up that way. "Well, you were wearing sunglasses. Inside. At night. Like Lenny Kravitz or Bono."

I burst out laughing. She managed a grin as the tension relaxed between us, and eventually laughed along.

"How's the lap?" she asked after a time.

"It's mostly healed up," I told her truthfully.

"You have no idea how sorry I am about that."

"No need to be." I flashed her one of my best smiles, the kind that women have swooned over ever since I was fifteen years old. "I will admit though, it's the hottest thing I've had in my lap in a long time."

Her cheeks flushed red and turned away from me as Phillip came back with a wrapped-up Christmas present. The rest of Christmas went by easier. At least Cara let me around her after that conversation. In fact, we talked a bit more, and I learned a lot about her.

I told myself that it would pass. Cara and Phillip's relationship would end at some point, and then I could swoop in and steal her. Sure, that would cause a scandal, but I'm Eric Celestro di'Vale. I'm used to scandals, and it would be worth it.

But it never ended.

They were together for four years, graduated from Oxford. She lived in Dubreva for a time, traveling the world, going to functions and events like a debutante. I could tell that it never settled well with her. She had the disposition of a homebody, someone who would rather sit down at a park and read, rather than make nice with diplomats.

I all but gave up on anything happening between us, even though I had subtly followed her in the literal and figurative sense. I turned to drinking more, slept around even more—anything to get her off my mind.

And now?

Now, I'm here with her in New Zealand. Phillip cheated on her. And she's at the far end of the house.

What are you waiting for?

I roll onto my side, towards the wall, away from Cara's direction. Even that little bit of movement takes a lot of effort, and I try closing my eyes to block her out. Focusing on unsexy things, like American corn dogs.

A scream rents through the house, and before I know it, I'm on my feet running towards Cara's room. The door is unlocked as I throw it open, the light from the hallway shining a beam into her room.

"What happened?"

She sits propped up against the headboard, her sheets wrapped around her body. She breathes heavily and tears fall from her eyes.

"Nightmare," she whispers. Her bottom lip trembles. "I dreamed he was with her. And many others."

I hesitate, wondering if this is a private moment for her and I should leave.

I stay.

She combs a hand through her hair and props the elbow on her bent knee. "I just...I just wish I knew *why*." Fresh tears fall. "I want to know why I wasn't enough for him."

I clear my throat. "It's not you, Cara. Never you."

Her gaze flicks up at me, her face woeful. Then it crumples and she hugs her legs to her chest, sobbing. My actions propel me forward again, and I sit next to her and gently put a hand on her shoulder, meaning to be a comfort.

She grabs me and buries her face into my chest, her sobs wracking her entire body. She's hurting. And there's nothing I can do about it.

I look up to see Herbert standing in the doorway. His watches us, and I wonder if he's going to say something or break this up. He knows what I should do, that I should stop being a shoulder for her to cry on, to stop this madness.

It's a train we can't stop.

He nods silently and pads down the hallway, leaving the two of us alone. Eventually, Cara's crying subsides and she falls asleep.

I don't sleep a wink.

This is not going to be a relaxing holiday.

9

CARA

I'm so fucking embarrassed the next day, I can't even look at Eric at the breakfast table.

I flick around my Kindle, trying to make myself look distracted, even though there is no internet. I'm not reading anything as I watch Eric to see if there's any awkwardness coming from him. I could just die of shame right here and now. Eric didn't need to see me like that last night. After all this, that's the last thing I needed to do.

So much for keeping that barrier up.

He doesn't mention it though, and is instead chatting with Herbert as the valet makes us breakfast. I can't listen to them over the pounding of my heartbeat in my ears and my compulsive counting, but I steal glances at their interactions as they laugh and talk to each other. There's a father/son dynamic going on between them, and I try to hide my smile.

"...Cara?"

My name crashed through my thoughts, the only word that has made sense all morning. I blink and look up. "Hm?"

"Do you want to go bungee jumping today?" Eric asks, presumably for at least the second time.

I stare at him, aghast. "What?"

The corner of his mouth quirks up. "Bungee jumping. You jump off a high point and spring back with cords—"

"I know what bungee jumping is," I say, annoyed. "But...*what*?"

Eric smirks and then turns his attention to Herbert. "Herbert, can you make a booking for us to go bungee jumping? The place where you dip your hands in the water at the bottom?"

I widen my eyes at how ludicrous that sounds.

"Yes, Sire," Herbert says. He nods towards me. "For two?"

Before I can answer, Eric steps in. "For two. Unless Cara doesn't want to go."

They both look at me, waiting for me to say otherwise.

I'm too stunned to say no. Usually in situations

like this, Phillip just makes the decision and I go along. But I'm a single woman and I can do whatever I want, whenever I want. "I'll go," I say, feeling a flash of pride at my new-found independence. And I'm fucking terrified.

"Very well then," Herbert says. "Two it is."

Eric gets a sly smile. "Join us, Herbert. I'm sure you'll have a blast."

"I'll sit this one out, your Majesty," the valet replies. "But thank you for thinking of me."

Herbert nods again and marches to the great room to make a call. Obviously getting the hint that Eric wants us to be alone.

And that may be the last thing I want right now.

The prime numbers rattle off in my head as I wait for Eric to speak. Finally, I look at him and he's watching me.

"Are you all right?" he asks softly.

"No," I say incredulously. "I'm about to go bungee jumping when I'm not sure I want to."

"You can say no at any time," Eric says. "No one is making you do it."

I nod. Still, somehow, I can't bring myself to turn him down.

"But what I meant is," he continues, "are you all right after last night?"

Am I? I wonder. After all, I cried in the arms of my ex-fiancée's brother. It's like something from a romantic comedy, except no one is laughing in my story.

It's strange, while I had bad dreams about Phillip on the plane over here, they were nothing like the night terrors I had last night. I kept seeing Phillip finding new women and assimilating them into his body, luring them in like an anglerfish, until he became this misshapen monster with all these heads of his paramours sticking out at various places on his body.

"*This is what you wanted, Cara,*" the Phillip-monster taunted as he reached out to me. "*You knew this when you agreed to marry royalty.*"

That was when I woke up screaming.

And then Eric came in and I held onto the only thing that made sense at that point. Except, what made sense last night confuses and worries me this morning. I remember the way Eric smelled last night, how his strong arms held me and just let me cry.

I'm so puzzled by all of this. Because what happened last night *felt right.*

And I don't know if that makes me any better than Phillip. Or the Phillip-monster from my dream.

"No," I admit truthfully. "I'm not all right." My hands are clenched and I have to make myself open them and set them in my lap. My breath shudders as I fight back tears. "I don't know what to do."

"Well," Eric says, "that's why we're here."

I nod. "I know."

"No, I don't think you do," he says. "What I'm aiming to do here, is to make you forget that asshole." He inches closer to me, the chair legs scraping against the floor. "I don't know much about advice. And I don't pretend to know what I'm doing. But what has helped me in the past when I've been depressed, is spending money. And I've got shitloads of money."

I laugh despite myself. "I can't ever repay you."

He watches me, his eyes sparkling, and I suddenly remember how the tabloid that called him the world's most eligible bachelor pointed out that he always appears starry-eyed.

"You've already paid me back, Cara."

I expect him to explain that further, but we're interrupted when Herbert comes back in the room at the most inopportune time. Eric sits back and tries to make himself look busy.

And me? I'm just as confused as ever.

"Booking confirmed, sire," Herbert says. "Shall I drive you and Miss Van Meter to the bridge?"

"Wait a second," I say. "*Bridge?*"

"I don't think I can do this," I say to the attendant.

"You got this," she says to me, encouragingly. I'm sure she gets this a lot.

I stand on a metal bridge overlooking a canyon that has a river cutting through it. The view is breathtaking, but that may just be because my lungs are paralyzed from fear. All I see are the rocks down below and all the many ways my body can break on them. All I have is a harness and a bungee cord made up of smaller elastics with frayed bits all down its length. It looks like a death trap. My mind quickly rattles off the maximum stretch rate for those bungee cords and if they won't stretch too much with my weight.

It seems perilously close.

I'm going to die here. I'm so going to die.

I hold onto the rail, and I squeeze my eyes shut as I make my way to the very edge of the ledge.

For once, I'm not counting prime numbers when I'm nervous. My brain is too scattered, too deep within the grip of terror to do anything other than wish I was anywhere else in the world.

Well, anywhere other than be in the same room as Phillip.

That one thought makes me snap my eyes open. I'm further out from the safety of the bridge than I realized. The wind whips around me, clawing at my New Zealand hoodie, even before I plummet towards the earth.

I'm cold.

And yet, I feel nothing. It's refreshing to not have that hurt inside me, even for the briefest second.

I look back at our group, and Eric stands there. His blue eyes watch me, and he's smiling encouragingly at me. To my utter surprise it gives me the strength to let go.

I don't fall gracefully. Hell, I don't even fall in style as Buzz Lightyear would say. But I plummet towards terminal velocity, screaming as I do. Time slows down, making my shriek stretch forever and ever.

My stomach is somewhere twenty feet behind me, and the wind is whipping my hair away from my face. Tears sting my eyes, and if I wasn't so wide-eyed, they'd blind me.

There's something very cathartic about putting

your life into relative danger after feeling like your world has ended. You realize that there's something else holding you onto this world.

My metaphorical tether just happens to be a bungee cord right now. In thinking that, now of all times, I'm also feeling a tether to a certain billionaire prince waiting for me on the bridge.

And when my fingers touch the water, it feels like a mini baptism, that I'm shedding the old me and reemerging as someone different.

It's a small step, but it's still progress.

Because, for once, I believe that I'll be all right.

10

CARA

Smiling comes easier after a couple of weeks in a winter wonderland. Life is good when you're able to unplug from the world every once in a while.

The three of us fall into a routine. We wake up, Herbert makes us coffee and breakfast, and then we choose an activity for the day. Some days that's reading. Other days, that's downhill skiing or snowmobiling, or renting a motorcycle and driving out to Wanaka, or renting a private boat and going out on Milford Sound. Or seeing the glow worms in Te Anau. There is plenty to do with Queenstown as our home base, even though I'm sure they're not the types of things that a billionaire prince would normally do. Yet Eric seems to enjoy it as much as me.

Herbert comes with us sometimes. Other times, he stays at the house, saying something about him being too old. I get the feeling that those quiet moments are as much of a vacation for him as this entire endeavor is for me.

Money is no problem, and while I can't contribute much financially (or even on credit), Eric obliges me when I want to buy coffees out or a snack to eat as thanks. It's a small thing, really, and I know it doesn't amount to much. But at least it makes me feel like I'm an equal by contributing to this whole thing.

After my attempt at cooking the first night, we eat out for dinner every night, and usually for lunch if we're out and about.

No one has recognized us and no one has come out to locate us from Dubreva. We're in our own fantasy bubble now. I count my prime numbers less often. And I stop believing that it is the end of the world for me.

Tears still fall, though. There is an empty hole in my chest where Phillip used to live, but the pain has faded to an ache.

I thought I was getting it all under control.

Until I woke up on my wedding day.

I'M FACING the wall when I feel the light weight of something being set at the foot of the bed.

"Miss Van Meter, your *uniform* has been washed and pressed," Herbert says. I never understood it; he always steams my hoodie and sweater. "And it's already ten in the morning."

"Thanks Herbert," I say through a mouth filled with thorns. "Just...leave them there."

I almost hear him hesitate. "Miss Van Meter, are you all right?"

I roll onto my back to look at the valet and through my film of tears, I can see him take a few steps back. "I made the mistake of looking at a calendar. I was supposed to be married today."

And I burst into fresh, inconsolable tears.

Sometime later—how much later, I don't know, because time seems to be both at a standstill and rushing forward at the speed of light—I feel a heavier weight on the edge of the bed.

"Cara?" Eric's voice. "Hey, Cara, look at me."

I'm almost too ashamed to do so, too afraid to show that all of this has been for nothing, that I'm still a wreck and nothing can put together the broken pieces of my soul. But after everything he's done for me, I look back at him, furiously wiping away my tears.

"Sorry. I didn't think...well, I didn't think this would be..."

"You don't have to apologize, Cara," he says. "Today would have been hard for you no matter what."

I watch the line of his jaw as it tenses up, and I wonder what he's thinking. *If* he's thinking of anything. There's a hardness to his expression. He's thinking deeply about something else, and the tension is making him as taut as a guitar string that's ready to snap.

Finally, he whips his head back to me and gives me a sad grin. "Let's change up the plans for today," he says. "Herbert! Cancel the boat charter."

"You don't have to do that—" I start.

The prince looks back his me, his eyes turbulent. "*We* are canceling going out on the lake. And," he pats my knee encouragingly "we're going to the bar to get fucking wasted."

I stare at him, incredulous. "But it's ten in the morning," I say, quoting Herbert's time earlier.

"And if there were ever an excuse to get

hammered at ten a.m.," he says, a sly grin coming onto his features, "it's the day you were supposed to get married to my asshole brother."

IT NEVER CEASES to amaze me what having a shitload of money does. It takes Herbert just a few phone calls, but we find a bar that, for a ten-thousand-dollar check, is willing to open four hours early just for us.

The place is a throwback to the American West, complete with deer heads on the wall and saddles for bar stools. Eric looks out of place here in his white linen shirt, tie, and pressed pants, but he chats with the bartender like he's always been here.

Meanwhile, I sit at the bar, looking glumly into my drink. At least the tears have stopped.

"Hey, Alice," Eric calls to the bartender, "How about a round of tequila shots?"

The blond bartender, who I think is sweet on Eric, gives him a wide grin as she ducks behind the bar. "You got it, boss."

I raise an eyebrow at the prince. "Shots?"

Eric takes my beer away and sips off the top. "I never figured you for a beer drinker."

I think back to all the times in college when I would nurse one beer throughout an entire party. I quirk a smile. "You're probably right."

"And this—" he indicates the IPA "—is not going to get you drunk anywhere near fast enough. So, shots it is. Until you can't even remember your own name. *That* is the best way to spend today."

Alice sets down shot glasses in front of us and starts pouring tequila with such gusto, the amber liquor is all over the place. We don't care though as we clink the glasses together and throw back the liquor, burning all the way down.

It dampens the pain and I smile at Eric. "Another one."

"If my lady demands it," he says, picking one up.

I try not to pay attention to him calling me, "my lady". I ignore the flutter that it gives me. Confusing, conflicting thoughts like those have no place here. Not when I'm mourning for what might have been with his brother.

I don't bring it up. And we drink.

Eric matches me shot for shot. I lose count of how many there are, but we polish off the lineup that Alice has set down in front of us, and work through another round. Speech slurs. Laughter comes easier. We clink our way through the different drinks, until oblivion numbs away that part of me that has died with Phillip's infidelity.

"I don't think I'll ever get married," I tell Eric somewhere between reckless and train wreck on the scale of drunkenness. "Not after all of this. Talk about overrated, right? What about you?"

Warning bells go off in my brain that I shouldn't bring this up. Not now and not with him.

Eric shrugs. I'm struck by how handsome he is when he allows himself to smile and let go completely. I realize now how guarded he keeps himself around me. The alcohol has broken down his barriers. Much like they're breaking down my own.

"I'm the world's most eligible bachelor," Eric says, giving me a lopsided smile. "Why would I ever give that up?"

"You're tied for the most eligible bachelor," I correct. "Phillip's back on the market. Unless he's already put a ring on that…other woman."

Eric's eyes darken at the mention of Phillip, and I watch as one wall comes up between us. "We both know that I inch just ahead, right?" he says.

"Of course," I say, trying to bring levity to where this conversation is going. "At least you don't pretend to be anything but what you are."

He casts his eyes down. "Oh, I pretend, Cara. I'm just so good at it, you don't know who I am otherwise."

I lick my lips and start stacking the shot glasses, doing anything to keep my hands busy.

"Phillip's good at it too," I say, unable to help myself from bringing up the man that broke my heart. "Maybe not as good as you—" Eric raises his glass to that "—but I always believed that he loved me."

"I think he did."

"I don't think so." My mouth keeps running and I can't stop it. And the words that come out next are the ones that have been eating me up inside. Ever since I met a certain crown prince in one of my classes at Oxford. "I mean, why would someone like Phillip fall for a math student from Missouri?"

Eric doesn't say anything. He doesn't even look my way.

Word vomit keeps spewing from my mouth in my attempt to cover up the uncomfortable pause. "After all, what do I know about his life? When he's grown up with...so much more than I had, what could I possibly bring him? The only thing I can think of is...simplicity? Or that I enriched his life in some way?"

"I think that's exactly why," Eric says softly.

"I was never going to be able to keep him, was I?" Fuck, there are fresh tears falling now. "I'm such a fool."

I comb a hand through my hair. When did the world start tilting? I think I'm about to be sick.

Eric leans forward and brushes a tear away from my cheek. I watch him, startled at the intimacy in the gesture. His eyes aren't connecting with my own. He's looking at my lips.

I freeze.

"Do you remember the first time we met?"

I try to smile, but falter. "How could I forget?"

His gaze is far away, looking back four years ago. "You had no idea who I was. When the entire restaurant knew that I was Eric Celestro di'Vale."

"I didn't even get a chance to know who you were afterwards," I say. "Pierre fired me and I was so damn embarrassed by the entire thing, I went straight home."

I sigh, remembering how scared I was about the whole debacle. I was afraid of being sued or worse. After all, there was that woman who spilled hot coffee from a drive-thru in the States. For a few weeks after that, I was sure that every phone call, every knock at the door was someone to arrest me for assault with hot liquid.

"I felt *awful*," I whisper.

The corners of his mouth pull up. "I wasn't angry," he says. "Rather, I was intrigued. Because, for once in my life, someone treated me like a human being and not some slingshot to power and fame."

"Normal people don't throw soup on each other."

"They also aren't you, Cara. There's something...*innocent*...about you. You tried your best to make it right. And you did." His eyes flick up to finally meet mine. He's seeing me now, his mind out of the past and in the present. Here, with me. "I looked for you after that, you know."

I gulp down some air. "You did? Why?"

His sits back, watching me with those blue eyes of his. "Because I wanted to have a normal conversation with you."

I try to laugh and falter as I wonder what's happening with my insides now. They're flip-flopping all around like fish on dry land. "I tried making myself un-findable at that point," I manage.

"I know." He chuckles softly. "But I wonder what would have happened if I had found you before you met my brother. I wonder if you would have fallen in love with me."

My lungs stop working as the seconds tick by, with us just watching each other. What am I supposed to say to that? Maybe I would have fallen for him? Maybe not?

I remember that night vividly. After all, I thought it was the end of the world for me. I remember seeing Eric in the restaurant, looking like a cocky asshole, wearing sunglasses inside. (Who wears sunglasses inside, right?) But I watched him from afar. With his dark hair and strong cheekbones, he was gorgeous. Magnetic. I knew that everyone in the bar noticed him. It was like he was in command of the world around him

Like a prince.

I wanted to speak to him. I wanted to pick his brain and see what was behind those sunglasses. And then I ruined everything by spilling soup on him.

Amazing how my clumsiness could ruin such a moment.

I find myself wondering what would have happened if things had worked out differently. Because at some point during this trip, Eric has become something more than Phillip's brother or the guy that had this crazy idea of going to the other side of the world.

And I'm only seeing it now.

I get up from my seat like it's on fire, trying to keep the space between us. I trip, but he catches me, steadying me with one arm. I feel the heat radiating off his body, a hot fire that I want to curl up next to. I want to press myself up against him soak up that heat, soak *him* up and more.

And I'm not like that.

I clear my throat and try to paste on that brave, unaffected expression. "Let's go back," I say. "I think I've had enough to drink."

"Are you sure?" He sounds surprised by this. Yet, all I want to do is go home so I can lay underneath the covers and nurse a hangover so I don't have to think about these conflicting emotions.

"Yes," I say. "I think I need to lay down."

Or something. Anything to keep myself from doing something I'll regret.

11

ERIC

I watch her as Herbert drives us back to the rental house. Her body language screams for me to stay away from her when all I want to do is...

What? Ruin this further? The alcohol is making my lips looser, and I've said too much already. The kind thing would be to take her back to America and end this. If today is any indication, she has emotional scars that are deeper than a holiday in paradise can repair, and all I'm doing is prolonging the inevitable. If not making it worse.

But I can't let it end here. Not when I just touched the tip of the iceberg that is my heart.

"Are you all right?" I venture.

She glances at me and nods after a beat. "Yes. I just need to lay down."

She said that back at the bar. It's almost like it's an excuse for her to separate herself from me.

"I'm not sure that you should be alone right now."

"I'm fine," she says. "Just too much to drink already."

I open my mouth to say more, but she turns away, effectively shutting down any further conversation.

We both feel the momentum of the limo stopping. She perks up, unbuckling her seatbelt and rushing out even before Herbert has a chance to open the door for her. I see her trudge up the steps to the mansion, unlock it, and go inside.

The door slam doesn't go unnoticed.

Herbert opens my own door, his expression perplexed as he watches after her. "I presume you told her your feelings, sire?"

"Not all of them, Herbert," I grumble, unfolding myself from the seat. "I just said that I wished I had found her before she met Phillip."

Herbert's face falls. "Your Majesty, you didn't. That poor girl."

"She *has* to know, Herbert."

"I told you not to break her heart. She is a fragile, wonderful creature, and you're—"

"Trying tell her the truth."

"And what do you expect will happen, sire? That she'll fall head over heels for you? Or that she'll believe—as I do—that this whole thing has been some sort of ploy for you to make her fall in love with you?"

Something akin to the former, although Herbert calling me on my bullshit has me grinding my teeth. That, swirled with the alcohol in my system is making me both belligerent and stubborn as hell. "That's not why I did this."

Herbert looks at me, unimpressed. "You may have started with good intentions, my prince. But that's not how it's ending, is it?"

I shake my head, feeling the fury rising inside me. "It doesn't end here."

I push past him and storm up the steps. Cara isn't the great room, meaning that she went directly to her bedroom. I ignore the alarms going off in my head, the ones that are telling me that I'm going too far that I should stop.

Yet I know that if I do, I'm going to lose her forever.

I try the door to her room.

Locked.

Fuck.

"Cara, open up," I tell her. "Cara, we need to talk."

"No we don't," I hear from inside.

I put my forehead against the hard wood and close my eyes. "Please open this door. You owe me that much."

At first, nothing happens. Then I hear the click of the lock and straighten up. The bedroom door opens just a crack and I see her tear-stained face glaring back at me. She's pissed.

"I don't owe you one fucking thing," she says through gritted teeth. "It was *your* decision to take me on this whole 'escape', as you call it. I wanted to go back home where I could hide from all of this and pretend like I had never heard of Dubreva or its royal family. It was your call to bring me here. I don't owe you anything for that. *Asshole.*"

That last word stings, and the alcohol-induced swirling in my head crescendos. She tries to close the door, but I jam my foot in the way.

"*I'm* the asshole?" I demand, angry myself now that she would categorize me that way. "I wasn't the one who cheated on you, sweetheart. In fact, I flew you halfway around the world so that you could escape from all of that for a bit. I've put you up in the nicest rental, took you out skiing, took you out to dinner every goddamn night—"

Her jaw is set as she glares back at me, refusing to back down. "Why?"

"Why what?"

"Why are you doing this? All for your brother's ex-fiancée?"

I stare at her, aghast. "Isn't it obvious?"

She falters, as if she's unsure of what to say next. I know because I'm the same way. "Tell me."

The command comes out as a whisper.

I comb a hand through my hair. How the fuck do you put feelings, pent-up for the past four years, into a simple explanation?

But I try, goddammit. I fucking try.

"I...*care* you about Cara. My brother always had everything; the crown, the media attention. The expectations. Fuck that. I never wanted any of that. But you... you were the one thing he had that I wanted. And now that you're not his..."

"So, that's it?" she asks, hurt edging into her voice. "I'm just a possession to both him and you?"

"No, that's not what I mean. Dammit, Cara, I—"

Words fail me. Hell, the whole universe fails me at this moment. So I do the only that comes to mind.

In one fluid movement, I force the door open further, grab her shoulders, and capture her lips with mine.

12

CARA

Oh. My. God.

Eric Celestro di'Vale—the second in line for the Dubrevian throne, billionaire playboy, and the younger brother of the man I was supposed to marry—is kissing me.

Thoughts about how wrong this is edge into my brain, about how this is something that some sort of gold digger would do, how this would be frowned upon by *everyone* in the world.

Yet, the longer he holds the kiss, the more it sweeps away all the other negative thoughts until one remains: *I want this so fucking badly.*

His lips consume me and I close my eyes, losing myself in it.

He breaks for air, his blue eyes heavy-lidded at

he looks down at me, stroking the sides of my cheek with his thumb. Waiting for me to make the next move, to give an indication that this is all right. He says one word: "*Cara*."

Like it's a prayer to him.

And it may be the alcohol affecting me, but fuck it all anyways. I'll probably regret this later, but holy hell, all I want is him.

Consequences be damned.

I grab the collar of his shirt and pull him to me, and he happily obliges as I bring him inside the room, the door closing shut behind us. In my room, there is no outside world to judge us. Only a man and a woman who are desperate to find escape in each other's arms.

He pushes me up against the door, and I gasp as at the contact. His hands cup my jaw as he worships my mouth. There's a sound coming from somewhere and I realize that I'm moaning against his lips.

He unzips my hoodie as I frantically undo his belt and begin to undo his trousers.

He laughs softly against my skin. "You're in a hurry, aren't you?"

"Less talking," I tell him coyly as I fight the zipper. I don't want him commenting on how unpracticed I am compared to him. I've only been with three guys in my life.

I feel him smile. "Yes, ma'am."

He obeys. Before his trousers fall to the floor, I see that he takes out his wallet and pulls a condom out, throwing it onto the bed. As a playboy, of course he'd carry condoms with him, and there's both jealousy and wonder that flares up through me about what that means.

He pulls my sweater over my head, and I shiver as the cold suddenly hits my bare skin. I suddenly wish I was wearing something sexier than two layers of touristy clothing. Even my bra and underwear aren't that exciting, but he doesn't comment on it. He doesn't even notice.

With practiced fingers, he undoes my bra, exposing my breasts to him. He massages one and tweaks my nipple, making it go immediately hard under his touch.

"You are so beautiful," he whispers, breaking my command, but in this moment, I don't care. "So fucking perfect."

I concentrate on keeping my breathing as even as possible, even though it hitches once his mouth covers a breast as he removes my jeans and panties in one go, and I kick them to the side. My own fingers are shaky as I undo the buttons on his white shirt, both afraid that I'll ruin it and that I'm somehow doing it wrong.

He chuckles and helps me the rest of way, exposing his sculpted, rock hard abs with a V that goes into his boxer briefs. Gently, I put my fingers underneath waistband of those boxers—and is that his own breath hitching as I do it?—and slip them off to the floor.

Now that we're both naked, I bite my lip to take just a moment to marvel at his body. He's an Adonis, a cliché unto himself, a man who is perfect in every way, all the way down to his well-endowed, erect cock.

There's fascination on his face as he watches me, just like I'm watching him. Like he's waiting for me to approve of what I see.

"*Cara.*"

My own name drives me wild. I can't take it anymore. I rock him onto his back on the bed, to which he gives a surprised gasp. As I crawl up on the plush mattress, he grabs the condom, tears it with his teeth, and unrolls it onto his length just before I straddle him, his cock pressing at my entrance.

"I like a woman who takes charge," he says appreciatively.

"I take that as a challenge," I say, just before I slide down his length in one slam. We both gasp at the movement, as I hold myself there, stretching to accommodate his size. There are no more words between us now, just this delicious heat that we're building up.

He grabs my hips as I ride him, his own hips bucking against mine. He thrusts in and out, the friction almost too much to take. His hands are everywhere I want them to be, on my breasts, holding me to him, or rubbing at my nub.

He pulls me to him, capturing my lips with his once again, just before the buildup is too much for me to handle.

I come, moaning his name into his mouth. He joins me a few heartbeats later, breaking the kiss to say my name again. This time, it's not a prayer, but a declaration as he empties himself into me.

For a moment, neither of us move, as if we're both afraid of what's to come next. I'm not feeling regret at what we did, it's just more or less I'm spent and the feeling of being loved wraps itself around me like a cocoon.

I lay my head on his chest, hearing his heart beat erratically as his arms come around to hold me to him. I could stay like this for the rest of my life.

"I've been waiting for that for four years," he rumbles beneath me. "*Four fucking years.*"

"I'm so sorry. I didn't know," I whisper. "I—"

"Shhh," he whispers. "Don't be sorry. Don't you ever be sorry." He lifts my chin up, our eyes connecting again. "It was worth the wait."

I find that I'm smiling at him.

"But," he says, "I wouldn't mind if I didn't have to wait so long to do it again."

13

ERIC

The sunlight streaming in through the window wakes me up out of the thick fog that has descended upon my brain. I wince and groan, blinking to turn away from the light, and reach out to cuddle...

Air.

Cara's side of the bed is empty.

I sit bolt upright and immediately regret it.

"Aw, fuck." I clutch at my head, which reminds me that I went to bed on the tail end of being drunk.

Oh no.

Did Cara wake up and was upset about sleeping with me yesterday? Through a pounding headache, I try thinking back to everything we did yesterday. We drank a lot at the bar, but when we got back to the house, we were sober enough to make adult decisions. Especially since we made that decision again and again and again. In fact, we didn't leave Cara's room at all since we got back yesterday afternoon.

Surely she didn't regret all that. Surely I didn't take advantage of the situation.

Surely I'm not some creep.

I get up, pulling on my boxers, with one thought in mind: find Cara.

Hopefully she's not on a plane back to America now (although how she would have the money for it, I'm not sure), bawling her eyes out over what we did. It meant everything to me. I don't think I could live through rejection like that.

I step out into the great room, and see Cara laughing with Herbert over a cup of coffee. She's wrapped up in one of the complimentary plush robes, looking beautiful, even though she's wearing no make-up or has otherwise gussied herself up.

And not to mention, this is despite the fact she should be hungover.

She notices me standing in my boxers, and for one moment, she doesn't react. Then, a brilliant smile transforms her face and she beams at me.

"Morning, sleepyhead," she says.

I stumble over towards the two of them, relief

spreading through me like a tidal wave. *She's still here.*

"How are you not hungover?" I groan, blinking at her.

She gestures to Herbert. "Your valet can make a mean Bloody Mary." Behind them, I notice an empty pitcher of the drink.

"I'll make another for you, Sire," Herbert adds.

"I appreciate it," I say.

"Plus," Cara adds, as my valet goes into the kitchen, "I drank a lot of water whenever I had the chance."

I frown. "You..." My voice trails off, as I remember seeing her drinking a glass of water in the bathroom, shortly before I fucked her up against the shower wall. I couldn't get enough of her yesterday. Still can't, as I look at the curve of her collar bone and I imagine running my tongue over that skin. I could take her right here, right now.

"You're a smart one," is all I can say.

She laughs and pats the seat next to her. In fact, she looks the most at ease that I've seen her since we got here. I did that. I trudge up and pull the seat back, ready to sit down when I notice a gift-wrapped package on top of the cushion.

I point to it. "What's this?"

Cara glances down, and then gives me a coy smile. "Something I got you while you were passed out. You were passed out for a long time. I saw it when I was shopping here the first day."

"What kind of stores did you go into your first day?" I say, grinning at her.

"Souvenir shops." As I pick it up and sit down, she leans into me, and whispers under her breath, "Open it where Herbert doesn't see."

This close to me, she smells like cucumber melon and something deeper that is all Cara Van Meter. I could bottle that scent and inhale it all day.

I glance at Herbert, making sure his back is to us as he preps the Bloody Mary. Not that he would mind being privy to anything Cara would give me. He's seen far worse, trust me. But I oblige her as I tear open the package, revealing...

Cara laughs, the gesture contagious and I'm chuckling along with her.

"A willy warmer?" I ask, pointing to the furry cock ring. "You saw this your first day and immediately thought of me?"

This catches her off guard and she swallows nervously with a shrug, as if she's trying to brush this off as innocent. "I, uh..."

I kiss her forehead. "Glad I was on your mind even then."

"I guess you were." She sits back and sighs, looking at her mug of coffee. "I got you that because I figured we needed some sort of levity after yesterday."

"Levity?" I frown. "Thanks, Herbert," I add as my valet sets a glass tumbler of my drink in front of me.

Cara looks uncertain about how to start, so I prompt her further. "You're thinking about what happens after this."

She nods. "I mean, what are we, Eric? Dating? Something more? Or is this just a fling that we're having before we go back to reality?"

Her questions hit me in the chest like daggers, but I know she has a point. We're in the midst of a scandal, the likes of which haven't been seen. I can't think of one time a commoner floated between a crown prince and his brother. Once the media gets ahold of this—and they will, this is such a juicy story for them—it will blow up like Justin Bieber's newest haircut.

Not to mention my mother's reaction to this. The very thought of that makes me ill.

It's too early with us to say anything definite. I know this, yet at the same time, I can't deny the attraction between us. I don't chase after things for four years without knowing in my gut that it's meant to be.

We're meant to be. And I can't pretend that it's going to be easy moving forward. But I'll take the brunt of everything and protect her as much as possible from the shitstorm headed our way.

I put my hand over hers, because I can tell that she's worried. "Cara, I—" *love* "—like you. And we'll figure this out, one step at a time."

"But—" she starts.

"Remember what I told you before we left Venice? That you should do what makes you happy?"

She blinks at me. "Yes."

"Well," I grin widely at her "does my cock make you happy?"

She laughs, embarrassed, and glances at Herbert, who just rolls his eyes. She's going to have to get used to my candid attitude around my valet. I know that Phillip is much more reserved. Then again, that didn't stop him from doing stupid shit.

Like letting her get away.

"Yes," she says. "Yes it does make me happy."

"We'll just take it one step at a time," I tell her. "You've got to give us a chance. Will you?"

She looks in my eyes and nods. "Yes."

"Good." I take a big swig of my Bloody Mary and grimace as I feel it go all the way down into my stomach. "Let's go to your room. I want to try this out."

I hold up the willy warmer and waggle my eyebrows. Herbert shakes his head in mock disapproval, and, luckily, Cara isn't too embarrassed to be carried back to her room.

14

CARA

We're both awakened by the doorbell ringing loudly and repeatedly. My limbs are entwined with Eric's. He hasn't slept in his room once in the week since we started having sex. Our days are filled with fewer outdoor activities, and more nights in so we can enjoy each other's company.

It's been bliss, paradise. I haven't thought about Phillip, not in the same way, since Eric and I started sleeping together. This whole thing doesn't make sense, not to the outsider. But when I'm in his arms, the world can go about its business; I have everything I need with him.

I don't want this to ever end.

It's almost scary, really, how I want to hold onto

this as much as possible. He's my billionaire prince, the one that I know I can depend on. I get the feeling that he cares about me, even more than I believed possible.

And I feel the same way towards him.

The doorbell won't stop ringing. I untangle myself from Eric, who groans as he rolls onto his side, burying himself into his pillow. After spending a few nights with him, I learned that he could sleep through the apocalypse if it meant that he could stay in bed.

I guess Herbert is his alarm clock as well as his valet. The thought makes me smile as I slip into my robe and pad out into the hallway. The ringing has stopped; I guess Herbert opened it to stop the rude, constant ringing, but curiosity gets the better of me, and I keep heading to the front door.

No one rings doorbells like that. Not unless it's an emergency.

"Herbert?" I call out. "Who is it?"

Herbert has stopped arguing with the visitor, just in time for me to round the corner. I freeze when I see who it is.

"*Phillip,*" I breathe.

The crown prince of Dubreva glares at me, at first, in disbelief, then his face falls and he pinches the bridge of his nose as he exhales loudly. He's the spitting image of Eric, and I almost forgot how closely the two brother resemble each other.

"So the rumors are true," he whispers. An accusation.

I wrap my arms around my waist as shame descends upon me. "What rumors?" I ask, even though I can guess what they are.

Phillip pounces on my question. "That you fled to the other fucking side of the world—with my brother no less—instead of waiting to talk to me about the, uh, news that came out."

"That you cheated on me?" I ask.

He flinches and averts his eyes. "It's...complicated."

I cock my hip, looking at him squarely. "Complicated how?"

Phillip's eyes meet mine, a darker blue than Eric's, imploring me to believe him or forgive him. The two are one and the same now, and I feel the temporary bandages that I have around my heart breaking apart.

I can't believe this. He's not the one who should be angry. "Cara?"

I turn to see Eric standing behind me in his boxers, bleary eyed from just waking up. His hair is all mussed up, looking achingly handsome in a way that is both adorable and sexy as hell.

Phillip sees him too, and the two brothers stare at each other for a long, shocked moment.

"*You*," Phillip utters, venom dripping from his voice.

"Cara get behind me," Eric says, striding forward forcefully.

I look at him incredulously, but he strides forward and sweeps his arm around me to put a physical barrier between me and his brother. I step aside, helplessly looking to Herbert for some guidance. The old man's face is pinched in confusion and wariness.

He knows what's about to happen. And, looking at it, I realize that there's only one way this is going to end.

"You've got some nerve showing up here," Eric growls.

Phillip laughs, nearly spitting at Eric. "*I've* got some nerve? You're the bastard who brought my fiancée halfway around the world."

"*Your* fiancée?" Eric thunders. "She stopped being your fiancée the second you stuck your dick in another woman."

"Oh, that's rich, coming from a man-whore like you," Phillip sneers.

"Sticks and stones," Eric taunts.

"See, that's your problem. You're like a giant, spoiled kid that wants his way." Phillip shakes his head. "You always wanted what I had, didn't you? From my toy cars when we were little, to the woman I was supposed to marry. You always wanted my things. *Always*."

"She's not something that you own," Eric corrects him. "And I love her."

I gasp at his words. Even though we've been sleeping together for a week and I've technically known him for four years now, it feels unexpected.

Eric notices my gasp and looks at me, his eyes burning all the way to my soul. "It's true," he tells me, almost apologetically. "From the moment I met you..."

I'm too shocked to say anything, but he shakes his head. This isn't the moment for us to discuss this further.

Yet, Phillip pounces on that, determined to hurt all three of us.

"Well, this is just great," the crown prince says, throwing his hands up in mock surrender. "That works out perfectly then. You get what I once had, Eric. And this gold digger gets what she wants."

The accusation makes the air in my lungs collapse, and it feels like all the life is squeezed out of my heart.

Something in Eric snaps. He tenses up and throws a punch, connecting with the crown prince's jaw, throwing the elder brother backward. An ear-splitting smash drowns out my cry, as Phillip disappears through the window frame and out into the snow embankment on the side of the house. I shout in protest as Eric storms across the room and steps over the window sill. A piece of glass nicks his calf, causing crimson to run down his leg, but he doesn't even notice it.

He's hellbent on making Phillip hurt, beyond reprieve.

With the two of them outside, I gesture to the valet to follow me. "Herbert, help me!" I cry as I slip on some snow boots.

"You might not want to go out there, Miss Van Meter!" the valet calls after me.

As soon as I set foot outside, I realize why. There are cars parked out in front of the house, some marked as Dubrevian diplomats, but there are other cars as well, news vans crowding the driveway. The media has found our little hideaway. A few men in suits try to keep the reporters and paparazzi at bay, pushing them back, but it doesn't seem to be doing any good.

A lot of the damage had already been done, but I just made it exponentially worse because they take immediate notice of me.

I shriek and hold up a hand as I'm blasted with flashes from all angles. Self-preservation tells me that I should run inside and close the door. There's another part of me, the responsible part of me, that forces me to continue my walk to the other side of the building, where Eric is pummeling Phillip with his bare fists. Even in his boxers, even in freezing temperatures deep in the snow, Eric has one thing on his mind: to get his brother to apologize.

A group of reporters are snapping pictures, documenting this moment for the whole world to see. I can imagine quite a few people who wouldn't want anything like that hitting the presses.

Then again, I'm out here in a robe, yelling at the brothers to stop. Like some gold-digging hussy.

"Eric!" I yell. "Eric, stop! *Please!*"

He either doesn't hear me or he doesn't care. Phillip has stopped trying to fight back and is now just trying to protect his face. I have to stop Eric before he kills him.

"Eric!" I shout again. "ERIC!"

That last time echoed all around us, and the prince hesitates. I manage to successfully grab his arm, pulling him off Phillip. Eric turns back to me, snarling, as if he's a wild animal, but stops. I must look frightened, because the anger on his face disappears like water draining into the desert.

"Cara," he whispers. He wraps me up in an embrace, as the rest of the world watches on, seeing me in the arms of another man.

"Just stop," I tell him. "Stop this."

Eric looks down at me, his expression hard before he nods. "You're right," he says, "you're right."

He lets go of me and staggers back to his brother who hasn't gotten up from his spot in the snow.

"If you apologize," Eric says to the form in the snow, "we'll bring you inside and get you patched up."

Phillip groans from his spot on the ground and manages to push himself up. He has two black eyes and numerous bruises forming on his face, and I'd be surprised if his nose isn't broken.

"Fuck you," he mutters as he winces and rubs his jaw. "You nearly killed me, you asshole!"

"You deserve a lot more than that," Eric says, his jaw clenched. "Now, apologize."

"I'm sorry you're an asshole," Phillip mutters.

"Not to me, you bloody idiot," Eric sneers. He gestures back to me. "To Cara."

That sobers up Phillip. His gaze falls on me and his anger dissipates as well. "I'm so sorry, Cara," he says slowly. "You have no idea how sorry I am."

He's talking about more than calling me a gold digger. He's talking about everything

I cover my mouth with both hands as I feel the tears fall, tears that haven't fallen since the day I was supposed to be married. I apparently still have a few left.

Eric watches me, his expression hardening before he turns back to his brother, offering him a hand up. "Let's get you inside before these bloodsucking paparazzi decide to make a straight-to-TV movie based on us."

15

ERIC

"How did you find us?" I demand, crossing my arms as I face my older brother. I note, rather proudly, that I've done a number on his face. He no longer looks like the pretty boy prince anymore. Aside from his fine wardrobe, he looks like any other punk who crossed a man in love.

That's right. I glance back to Cara, who hasn't said much since we got back inside the house and curtained off the window. She's been sitting by herself at the kitchen island, watching Jarvis, Phillip's valet, fuss over him and bandaging up his cuts. The valet glares at me the entire time, and I remember why I don't like him.

My brother, meanwhile, is glaring daggers at me

through his one open eye. He holds an ice pack over the other one that's swelling shut.

"I should call the cops on you for assault," Phillip mutters. He sounds like he's in pain. Good.

"But you won't, because of media scandal," I say, calling his bluff.

Phillip scoffs. Yeah, we've all caused enough scandal to last for generations, so he won't do shit.

"So, again," I say more forcefully, "how did you find us?"

"You really think it's that hard?" my brother says, glaring at me. "Especially in this day and age?"

We haven't been online once, our phones are turned off, and I've been avoiding recognition as much as possible. "We were very careful."

"Yeah, well, so was I," he says quietly.

To my left, I hear Cara's sharp intake of breath. Maybe I don't want her to hear this. Maybe this will touch on some open wounds that don't need to be opened again.

"Basically," Phillip continues, "it comes down to this: I knew you were in New Zealand for the last three weeks. I didn't think much of it—fuck, I thought you were avoiding the frenzy as much as possible." He combs a hand through his hair. "Because you avoid responsibility like the plague.

You just always did what you wanted without consequences or recourse."

"That's not true," I mutter.

Phillip rolls his eyes. "Meanwhile, I thought Cara had gone into hiding. I checked her home in Springfield—your parents are livid with me, by the way, almost as much as they're worried about you." He looks at Cara. "Then someone snapped a picture of you guys at Milford Sound last week. And that's making its rounds on the tabloids, by the way."

I curse under my breath. Even on the other side of the world, we can't escape the public eye.

My brother snickers. "I thought, 'Surely, that's not true'. Why would Cara have anything to do with Eric? I mean, they hardly know each other. What would she be doing with him?" He sighs. "I didn't believe it. Not until I saw you standing here, in this house, Cara. And I think Eric's reaction confirmed my worst fear."

"Which was?" Cara asks.

"That I lost you forever," Phillip says.

Cara licks her lips and she lets out a low breath. "You lost me when you cheated on me."

"It was a mistake," Phillip says.

"A mistake?" she says, her voice turning shrill.

"Sleeping with another woman is a *mistake*? Throwing away my heart is a *mistake*?"

"That's not what I meant, Cara," he tells her.

"You could have tried calling me as soon as the news broke," she tells him. "Yeah, sure, I left Venice in a hurry—I was there for my bachelorette party, because we were supposed to be married—"

"Last week," Phillip murmurs sadly. "We were supposed to be married last week."

"—but I had my phone with me for about three hours. I cried, holding that phone, wishing that you'd call to tell me that it was a lie. That everyone was misinterpreting it. That she was just a friend or anything else rather than the worst case."

"It was the worst case," Phillip tells her. "And I can't tell you enough how sorry I am for that." He reaches out to clasp her hands in his, but she flinches and scoots away from him.

This feels like an incredibly private conversation, one that I shouldn't be privy to. Especially since they're talking about what to do next with their futures. What am I hoping for? That Cara will stand up and declare her love for me and we'll live happily ever after? Not right now, and maybe not ever. This isn't a fairy tale.

This whole thing is fucked.

Wondering what I should do, I glance at Herbert, who shrugs. He's at as much of a loss as I am.

I glance back at Cara and Phillip. She's glaring at him, and he looks hurt, not just physically, but emotionally as well. I hate the pain in Cara's eyes, her own hurt radiating from those green eyes that I've come to love.

"So what happens next?" I find myself saying, doing anything I possibly can to break up the tense moment.

Phillip looks back at me and sighs, pinching the bridge of his nose. I hate that I do the exact same thing, like I'm immediately guilty of all his sins by being his younger mirror. I make a mental note to never do that again.

"We have to head back to Dubreva," Phillip says. "We have to figure out how to proceed, present a press statement, get Mother to pull a few strings. Anything." He sits forwards and rubs his hands together. "We have to repair this scandal. We have to make things right."

"I don't know if there's any way to fix this," Cara tells him.

He looks back at her. "We have to do *something*."

"Wow, they really are being bloody cruel," I say to Herbert as we're heading to the airport. We're about to fly my plane back to Dubreva to sort through this whole ordeal. I scroll through social media on my phone. News that Cara was with me this entire time is blowing up the internet.

Herbert glances at me in the mirror. "Try to not let it bother you, Sire," he says apologetically. "I know it's hard."

That's a gross understatement.

The media are calling it the scandal of the century. I'm being labeled the playboy who stole the crown prince's fiancée—which, I have to let slide, or else I'd punch through the limo window. But they're being especially petty to Cara, calling her things she doesn't deserve, things that make me want to kill whoever made these assumptions.

She's none of those things.

In fact, everyone is being strangely kind to Phillip. While there are some who are applauding Cara and I for "getting back at Phillip" after his infidelity, most are being sympathetic to Phillip's cause, saying that we were most likely sleeping together *before* Phillip was caught in Paris with that brunette and that him cheating on Cara was some sort of revenge sex.

Some people have wild imaginations.

But either way you slice it, we're fucked, and I can only hope that Cara hasn't turned on her phone yet. For some inexplicable reason, she decided to fly back to Dubreva with Phillip. Okay, maybe it's not inexplicable and they'll have plenty of time on the plane to work through their differences, but I can't help but think that she'd be better off in my plane where she can gather herself. Close by the ones who love her.

Oh, and the cherry on top? As I was packing up my clothes in the rental house, Phillip told me that he and the brunette, "Julie", aren't together anymore.

It was a onetime fling. In his mind, that's forgivable, because it didn't mean anything.

I wanted to use him as a punching bag again.

After seeing too much vitriol and hatred, I toss the phone away in disgust. I can't take this anymore, and I know this is just the start. I look out the window, seeing the mountains pass by. It's amazing how your own personal world can be crumbling, but the rest of the universe can go on like nothing ever happened.

These mountains are millions of years old. I'm sure they've seen worse scandals.

I should take solace in that fact, but I'm not.

Instead, I'm worried about Cara being alone with Phillip on the plane. Worried that she'll fall for his excuses and forgive him.

I close my eyes, wondering if there is anything I could have done differently in the past few weeks that would have changed this outcome. Despite the heartache that will come after this, I wouldn't have traded it for all the money in the world.

I love her. And even a few weeks in heaven is preferable to life lived in World's-Most-Eligible-Bachelor Hell.

The car slows, and I look up, realizing that we've made it to the airport. Herbert turns around in his seat. I blink at his expression. For once, the old man looks remorseful. Fatherly, even, which is unusual for him.

"Your Majesty," Herbert says. "I know it's not going to be easy from here on out. I was against this from the outset, but seeing you with Cara over these past few weeks has really opened my eyes."

"To what?"

He smiles warmly at me. "To what truly makes you happy in life. Don't give up hope, Sire. It will work itself out."

"I hope so." I feel the back of my throat close up from the swell of emotions. "Thank you, Herbert."

"You're welcome, your Majesty."

I chuckle mirthlessly. "Why not call me Eric? After all, I could really use a friend right now."

"And that, Sire—*Eric*—I can be for you. A friend"

Now the emotions are coming through and I reach through the privacy window to give my valet an awkward hug. We stay like that for a few moments. I hold onto him like he's the last connection I have to this life.

"All right," I say, sitting back, trying to compose myself. "Let's get this over with." I put on the playboy mask that I have, that cocky, arrogant, ne'er-do-well smile that shows that I don't give a fuck what anyone thinks.

I may have to wear it for the rest of my life.

I take a steadying breath. "Hope you're ready for another long-haul flight, Herbert."

"Always, Eric."

16

CARA

I can't help but compare Phillip's private jet to Eric's. Funnily enough, I'm not sure what that means for me, whether I'm getting used to this lifestyle and it's losing its luster.

Might not have much of this anymore.

I chuckle self-deprecatingly. What a mess. I haven't turned on my phone yet, and I may just exit all social media and news for the next fifty years to escape the world's assessment of me.

They have no idea who I am and what I went through. They don't care that I loved Phillip and that I...

Love Eric?

I bite my lip, trying to decide my complicated feelings towards him. I could tell that he was hurt when I decided to fly back with Phillip. The two of us need to talk. And I need to make a decision for myself for once.

"It always drives me wild," Phillip says, "when you bite your lip like that."

I look at the crown prince. He's sitting in the seat opposite me, a martini in hand as he watches me. A drink. That's what I need right now.

I don't order one.

"It's my thinking face," I tell him.

He smirks. "So you always bite your lip when you're counting your prime numbers?"

I told him that fact about two years into our relationship, because he asked me why I get this faraway look in my eyes sometimes. Come to think of it, I haven't been counting prime numbers in a long time. Almost like my anxiety and my awkwardness are gone.

Eric brings me peace.

"You're still biting your lip," Phillip tells me.

"I've got a lot to think about," I tell him. "*We've* got a lot to think about."

Phillip nods. "Yes," he agrees. "Yes we do."

"What happened, Phillip?"

Even though he must have been prepared for it, I

watch as his bravado falls and he closes his eyes, considering his next comment.

"I got scared," he admits quietly. "The idea of marriage. Of locking down everything, saying that's *it* for me. For the rest of my life."

"Ouch," I say out loud, genuinely hurt.

He shakes his head. "No, that came out wrong. It has nothing to do with you and everything to do with this constant pressure that I have. Ruling a kingdom. Making diplomatic treaties, showing up at political functions. Making sure the bloodline continues." He looks pointedly at me. "Getting married."

"You didn't have to propose, Phillip," I tell him. "Hell, I'm not even sure I was ready for marriage."

I surprise myself with that last comment. Because, while I've never considered that before, it suddenly popped out, and I realize it's true. I wasn't ready for marriage.

Because, maybe, it's been to the wrong prince all along.

Shit.

Phillip is nodding along with me, his own train of thought mirroring mine. "Right."

"Right." My heart pounds with that revelation,

and I swallow thickly to try to keep it in my chest. "So who was she?"

He knows exactly who I'm talking about. "Her name is Julie. She's a reporter for *Le Metro*, a French newspaper. You went off to your bachelorette party, and I...well, I panicked. I had an exclusive with her in Paris, so I went, and one thing led to another, and—"

"I know the rest," I say.

"No, you don't." He reaches out and clasps my hand. This time, I don't shirk away from his touch. It doesn't give me the warm fuzzies like it used to. Like Eric's touch does to me now. "I thought I knew what I was doing. Those pictures that you saw of me in Paris? I thought I was making my stance known that people shouldn't ever fuck with me. That I was still in control of my own destiny. I'm a prick and I'm so goddamn sorry for it. I woke up the next morning, alone and with a thousand and one regrets."

I don't say anything. I *can't* say anything, not in relation to that. Eric's assessment of Phillip's behavior was dead-on.

"I hurt you, Cara. And I'm so, so sorry about that."

"Are you still with her?" I ask.

He shakes his head with a laugh. "No. She ran

her own expose after that. Saying that I was severely lacking in the crown jewels department."

From my own experience, I know that he doesn't compare to Eric. A memory of the younger prince with the willy warmer—yes, he wore the damn thing, and I'll probably laugh at that mental image for the rest of my life—flashes in my mind.

I don't mention that though, although Phillip knows me well enough to know that I'm embarrassed. "What?"

"Nothing," I say, shaking my head. "Nothing at all."

For one moment, Phillip looks uncomfortable and he sits back, letting go of my hands. "Can I ask you a question?"

"Shoot."

"How did it happen? Between you and Eric?"

I smile at him. "You always treated me like a princess. He treats me like his equal."

Phillip blinks as he processes my comment. "I guess this means that we can't go back to the way we were," he says.

I shake my head. "Even if I hadn't gone to New Zealand with Eric, even if I hadn't fallen for him—that wouldn't have been an option from the second you slept with her." My voice cracks. "I loved you and you hurt me, Phillip."

"You have no idea how much I regret that."

"Yes," I say softly, thinking back to spilling the soup on Eric's lap back at Le Petit Cochon. I regret that action. I regret running away. I regret not getting to know him first and keeping my heart protected. "We all have our regrets, don't we?"

We sit in silence for a few minutes before a thought strikes me.

"Oh! By the way…" I reach into my purse and take out my wallet. I pull out Phillip's American Express Black and hold it out for him. "This is yours."

Phillip bursts into laughter. "And here I was thinking about cancelling it," he says. He takes it from me and peers down at it, almost like he's dubious of it.

"I didn't use it."

"I know you didn't. I was watching to see where you would have tried using it, so I could have located you."

I shake my head. "It wasn't mine to use when we were no longer together."

He nods as he puts it back into his own wallet.

"So I'm guessing Eric bought you this get-up?" he asks, pointing at my hoodie and sweatshirt.

"I paid for it." Or rather, I put it on credit, but I'm not splitting hairs. "I tried contributing as much as possible."

Phillip nods, and offers me a sad smile. "You would have made a good queen, Cara."

I shake my head. "No," I admit. "I would have made a great *partner*."

"Yes," he says remorsefully. "Yes, you would have."

IF QUEENSTOWN IS A WINTER WONDERLAND, Dubreva is a Mediterranean paradise. I watch the small island country from the sky, with its colorful buildings cut into the side of the mountains amongst the turquoise-blue sea.

The country is small, about the size of Connecticut back in the States, but there's an ancient history and wonder here that dates back to ancient Greek times. There are modern skyscrapers on one side of the island, the tiny metropolis acting as one of the world's largest centers for trade, but the rest of the island is a vacationer's paradise.

I'd never even heard of the country until I met Phillip in one of my classes at Oxford, and I never realized how big of a role this country would have on my life.

I close my eyes, waiting for the impact of the tires on the tarmac and for us to stop. My hands shake, and I feel lightheaded from the stress and worry about what's next.

I'm going to be here, by myself for one more day. As he's flying his private jet back himself, Eric won't be here for another 24 hours.

I almost envy that he gets to delay the inevitable.

Phillip peers at me. "Are you ready for this?"

No. "Yes."

We unbuckle our seatbelts and stand. I make sure to put as much distance as possible between us. They don't teach you how to deal with scandal and the press when you become engaged to a prince. And they also don't teach you how to deal with the fallout when the relationship doesn't work out.

My best defense? I put on huge sunglasses and wrap a scarf around my head. I used to wonder why celebrities did stuff like this. Now I completely understand why. Because even though the paparazzi will recognize who I am, it will at least cover up my tears as they fall.

Phillip catches my hesitation. "I'll go first," he tells me as he smirks sadly. "Just don't make any comments. Don't make eye contact. Don't do anything that draws attention to yourself. We'll head back to the palace where we'll get all this sorted out."

He turns away as I feel my stomach drop into my toes. I can't do this. There's no way I can face all of what's coming my way. I went to New Zealand to escape all of that, and here I am, facing it.

Phillip disappears out the door, going down the stairs. I hear the flurry of photographs being taken and the questions being shouted at him. Most of them are about me, and there are some awful, prying ones that no one has the right to know.

A bodyguard joins my side and I look up at him, wondering what he thinks of this entire thing. If he is judging me, he doesn't show it.

Here goes nothing.

I suck in a deep breath, and step out. The scattering of flashes catches me off guard, and I stagger for a moment, trying to get used to it. The onslaught is endless as I make my way down the stairs to the waiting limo.

"Cara! Is it true that you slept with His Royal Majesty, Eric?"

"Miss Van Metter, were you really with the younger prince in New Zealand this whole time?"

"Can I get a comment about your feelings regarding Prince Phillip's infidelity?"

So many questions as microphones are shoved in my face. I slowly make my way to the limo. The bodyguard intercepts most of them, pushing them away from me. My heart pounds in my ears, panic threatening to overtake me.

Phillip did this. I can do it too.

After what seems like hours, but could have been only thirty seconds, I reach the open door and slip inside. The bodyguard closes the door and I manage to breathe a sigh of relief as the limo speeds away.

Then I turn to see Phillip sitting across from me, ill at ease. And beside him is his mother, Her Royal Majesty Queen Victoria IV, ruler of Dubreva and one of the most powerful monarchs in the world.

And she's glaring right at me.

"Well, well, well," she says, giving me a predatory smirk. Her eyes glitter with fury, and to be honest, I don't blame her. "Whatever shall we do with you?"

17

CARA

Well, that could have gone better.

In fact, the only way it could have gone worse is if the queen had thrown me in jail. It was a fine time to learn that they have the death penalty here, too.

I'm in our room—Phillip's room, I guess now, since we're no longer together—clearing out all my things. I've spent the last two years here, living the life of a princess. There's not much that's mine, but I still sort through it all.

It's really fucking hard. I try to do it with an impassive face, to prove to myself that I'm not breaking up inside.

I never did get along with Phillip's mother. She never wanted her son to marry a commoner, especially a math student from America. She probably had political alliances lined up for him, ready to move Dubreva to the international spotlight.

Well, I certainly put it in the spotlight, as much as Victoria didn't want it that way. I'm still burned by her fury with me.

It's probably well deserved. I know I'll remember the conversation every day for the rest of my life.

"I want you out of this country," she told me as the limo wound its way through the tightly packed streets of Dubreva. "I don't care where you go from here, but you're not welcome here. Ever again."

I froze. I expected some sort of retaliation from the Queen herself, but nothing like this. Maybe anger, being yelled at, name calling. But certainly not deportation.

"Mother," Phillip chided.

His mother whirled on him, anger flashing in her eyes. "None of this would have happened if you would have just married Alexandra Daae like you were meant to."

"I fell in love," Phillip defended himself.

"And look at what love did," Victoria snarled, gesturing to me. "You sticking it where you shouldn't —really, I *expect* it from Eric, but not you, Phillip—

and this common whore sleeping with your brother."

I bristled at the accusation. "Don't you dare judge me," I told her. "Don't you dare act like you know exactly what happened."

"And don't you dare tell me what to do in my own country, young lady," Victoria said. "You don't understand any of the implications of what you've done."

"I loved Phillip," I told her. "He was the one who broke my heart."

Phillip winces at that.

"Obviously," Victoria sneers, "you're some sort of social climbing whore who is just interested in my sons for the status."

"You truly think that?"

"Absolutely," she said with a dismissive wave of her hand. "So, you are to be deported from my shores the second you get your things packed. You're lucky I'm even letting you do that. You're cut off, no more communication with my sons. Ever."

"Mother," Phillip said again.

"And if I refuse?" I asked blithely.

Anger flashed in Victoria's eyes. "If you don't leave or otherwise disobey my command, I will throw you in jail where you'll never see another sunrise."

Okay, it was starting to get scary. "And what if one of your sons contacts me? What am I supposed to do then?"

"They'll know better."

"Eric said he loved me, you know."

"Eric?" Victoria threw her head back and laughed. "And you're basing your plans off that? Eric loves anything with breasts."

"I love him too," I whispered.

Those words rang true the second they left my lips. It was crazy, really, how quickly that happened. At some point, from my nearly burning him with hot soup to flying out to New Zealand, I'd fallen in love with the billionaire prince.

And this bitch wanted to take it away from me.

I remember Victoria seething at me. I remember the way her hands clenched and unclenched, like she was having to restrain herself from reaching across the seats to strangle me.

"I don't know what kind of spell you're able to cast over my sons," Victoria said in a low, dangerous voice, "but you will leave Dubreva as soon as possible."

And that's how I ended up in my room, packing.

True to my first inclination, I only have a few mementos here that are mine. Everything that Phillip had given me is still on their hangers and tucked away in drawers. No use in incurring more of the queen's wrath by leaving his room messy.

A bodyguard stands at the door, watching me. In case I'll steal something or try to flee maybe, although I can't be sure.

I shoulder my backpack and look around the room. It's sad to think that the only things I'll take with me from the last four years fit inside one backpack. Life is defined by experiences, but I'll have so little physical evidence to remember all this by.

Proof that I once loved two princes. And that I still love one.

"Time to go," the bodyguard says in a pseudo-Arnold Schwarzenegger voice.

I hesitate, fighting the tears. It feels wrong not saying good-bye to Eric. He's arriving tomorrow, but the queen is ushering me out before I even have a chance to tell him how I feel. Not when I've only just realized it.

"Can I leave a note?" I ask.

This catches him off guard. "A note?"

"Yes, a note." I slip off the backpack and take out one of my notebooks from my years at Oxford. I grab a pen, one of those cheap pens you get and I'm surprised at how how long it has been since I last used one. At first, the pen doesn't work, but I manage to get some ink out of it and scribble a note.

I fold it up and tuck it into my pocket, afraid that the bodyguard will suddenly decide that I can't write a note and take it from me. I quickly zip up my bag and grab it.

"All right, I'm good to go."

Even though I know I won't ever be.

We walk down the hallways, heading towards the front where I'll be escorted to the airport. It's only a puddle jumper to get me off the island and into central Europe. From there, I'm on my own. I have no idea what I'll do, as I don't even have a cell phone to call my parents or friends.

My heart pounds, hoping that I'll either pass by Eric's room or see Phillip. I must leave this note.

The more time that passes, the more it feels like I won't get my chance.

Once I see the front door, it feels like all hope is lost. *No.* I've missed it. Missed my chance to—

"Cara!"

I turn to see Phillip jogging to the foyer. To say bye or to tell me something, I'm not sure which. I've just never been so glad to see him.

"Cara, I'm so sorr—"

He doesn't get another word out as I rush up to give him a huge hug, effectively squeezing all the air out of his lungs. He stands there for a shocked moment but then wraps his arms around me.

"I'm so sorry," he whispers.

"Thank you for everything," I tell him softly, and I feel him stiffen, confused at my words. As surreptitiously as I can, I slip the note into his trouser pocket. He pulls back to look down at me, his question unspoken.

"Please give that to Eric," I tell him. "It's important."

The bodyguard clears his throat, my countdown getting ever closer to zero. Phillip's expression is still that of bewilderment, but he nods.

I guess that's as good as I'm going to get.

I turn to leave, ready to face the cameras again and do my walk of shame back to America. However, that's going to happen with a half-filled credit card and no way of contacting my family.

It's only when I'm on the small plane from Dubreva to Athens that I finally let the tears fall. And they don't stop until long after I land.

18

ERIC

She left me a note.

On a torn sheet of journal paper, no less. How very Cara-like of her.

I hold it in one of my hands, debating if I should open it and read it, or save it. I stand in the hallway where Phillip cornered me shortly after arriving. All I know is that Cara is no longer in Dubreva. My mother kicked her out of the country. And I arrived a day too late to stop it. A part of me is furious with Phillip that he'd let Mother get away with deporting the poor girl.

Then again, I know how ruthless our mother can be. It's how she keeps the European Union and other interested countries from absorbing us like a sponge.

But I would have stood up to Mother.

Cara should have stayed with me. I could have protected her from that.

"Open it, you idiot," Phillip tells me.

I glance at him, noting how he still sports a shiner from where I punched him back in Queenstown. Otherwise, the rest of his face is healing nicely.

"You read it, didn't you?" I ask.

Phillip shrugs. "Of course, I did."

I sigh in annoyance.

"When a woman puts a note in your pocket to give to your brother," Phillip says, "wouldn't you read it too?" When I don't answer, he grunts in irritation, reaches out and opens it for me.

There's not a whole lot to the note, but in it is my whole world.

I love you. You are the 3/5 to my 2/5. You brought me my happily ever after. - C

I stare at it for the longest time. All thoughts leave me. Everything I'd ever hoped to hear from Cara is here. Everything. And now, I'm not sure what to do about it.

"That's more than she ever said to me," Phillip says, breaking into my thoughts.

"What?"

He points to it on the sheet of paper. "The happily ever after part. She never said that to me."

I reach up to pinch the bridge of my nose, but at the last moment, I turn it into running my hands through my hair. I'm trying to be as different from my brother as possible. I'm my own person.

"Obviously, you didn't bring her happily ever after," I say.

"Are you?"

The point-blank question gives me pause. "Am I what?"

"Going to give her that happily ever after?"

I look at Phillip, wondering where this new version of my older brother came from. This one is more spirited, more hopeful, less world-weary than the one I last met. There's remorse, sure, because his life is just as turned upside down as mine.

But I can tell that he's rooting for me. Even though I gave him that black eye and nearly broke his nose.

Decision made. Even if it meant the world falling apart around me.

"I'm going to damn well try," I say, turning away from him and striding down the hall. I can almost feel Phillip's grin at my back as I keep walking. He's proud of me.

"Tell her I'm sorry, again," he yells.

I turn and walk backwards for a few paces as I shout back, "Sorry about the black eye."

Phillip's expression turns grim and I laugh as I start jogging down the hallway.

"Herbert?" I ask, as my valet falls into step with my near-run.

There's mischievous glee on the old man's face. He doesn't even seem winded. "Yes, Eric?"

I've managed to get him to stop calling me "sire" or "Your Majesty", but there's still something so formal about the way he addresses me. It makes me grin widely.

"Call the airport and get the jet prepped," I tell him. "We're flying to America."

Missouri. I literally have no idea where Cara lives beyond that, but I'll comb the entire country to find her. And if she's not there, I'll search the rest of the world. It's amazing what a billion dollars can help you find.

"Right away, Eric," Herbert says, taking out his cell phone.

I have nothing packed—hell, where I'm going, I don't need anything. I just need to get there and end this. Sweep her off her feet and use that old American adage of riding off into the sunset with her. I'll—

"Where are you going?" a familiar voice thunders.

I slow as my mother intercepts me in the hallway, carrying herself with all the elegance and grandeur of a peacock. She's certainly preening like one too.

"You can't stop me, Mother," I tell her with a shrug. I can't keep the grin from my face.

I see the fear run through her eyes, and I know exactly why. She could always control Phillip, ever since we were kids. He was the goody two-shoes who wanted to impress her. And I was always the rebel, defying her every chance I got. Phillip proposing to Cara might have been a middle finger to our mother, but she tolerated it, at least.

Until now. And she's not going to like what I have to say about it.

So I keep jogging.

"Eric!" she says to me. "Eric, turn around and address me when I'm talking to you! I'm your mother, the queen!"

I stop and face her, giving her that last request. "What do you want?"

She doesn't answer my question. Rather, she

bustles up to me to glare at me, eye to eye. "You're going after her, aren't you?"

"Of course."

"No, absolutely not." She shakes her head vigorously. "I forbid it."

I chuckle. "You forbid it?"

"I'm your queen, as you'd like to forget."

"And I'm my own person. And I'm going to live my life." I turn to leave.

"With that harlot?"

Calling Cara that fucking pisses me off, even if it is coming from my own mother. I narrow my eyes. "That 'harlot' is the woman I love. Sure, our lives may not be perfect. But..." I grin. "Nothing ever is. And I don't have to follow your command. You can't stop it."

With that, I do leave with her shrieking after me. "Eric, if you leave, you're not welcome back here, ever again!"

"Frankly, Mother," I tell her, flipping the bird, "I don't give a damn."

19

CARA

"Cara, are you coming inside?"

I look up from my Kindle to see my mother sticking her head out the front door as she looks at me, a worried frown on her face. I'm on the front porch of my childhood home back in Springfield and it feels…so damn normal after everything that's happened. I never thought of home as a farm, but after everything, it certainly is quaint.

I shift my feet to push the porch swing a bit more. The evening air is hot and sticky, but it feels like home to me. And it's the only safe-haven I have now.

"One more chapter," I tell her, holding up the e-reader. "I have to see if Tyler ends up with Kade in the end."

Because happily ever after only happens in books. I learned that the hard way.

Mom's face pinches into a deeper frown, but after a week of my melancholy, she knows better than to ask.

"All right," she says dubiously. "But come inside before the mosquitos eat you up. And I'll save you some apple pie."

Mosquitos and apple pie. Seriously, what a slice of Americana.

She shuts the door leaving me to myself. Which is just fine.

I've been home for a little over a week, after a horrible, disastrous journey back to the States. I landed in Rome, and ended up jumping on a public computer to my social media channels (and pointedly trying to escape any news about me) to find any friend who was online that would listen. I managed to get ahold of Suzi and Giorgia and Christabel and they managed to wire me some money. I owe them something like €2500 for my plane ticket home. Hopefully I can find a job as a professor soon and start paying them back.

Granted, I have no idea who would hire someone who graduated from Oxford two years ago and never worked as a teacher in her life. But I'll figure it out.

"Everything has a way of working out," I mutter as I flick to another page in the book.

I can't get Eric off my mind. He's the last thing I think of before I go to sleep and the first thing I think of when I wake up in the mornings. And after just one week of sleeping next to him, my bed feels woefully empty without him.

I miss him, goddammit. And there's an ocean and his fucking psychotic mother keeping us apart.

Headlights on the road blind me momentarily, and I blink, looking up at the delivery truck. A quick look at the time on my Kindle says that it's nearly seven, far too late for delivery.

Then they turn down the driveway, pulling right up to the house.

I frown, slightly irritated to have my reading interrupted further, but I switch off the Kindle and pad down the steps to meet the driver as the door opens.

"Are you Cara Van Meter?" the man asks in a gruff voice as he looks down at his clipboard, a package underneath his arm.

"I am."

"Package for you. Sign here."

Confused, I sign the clipboard. He then thrusts

the package into my hands. I look down at it, and gasp lightly.

It's from Dubreva. A small, light package that is more of an envelope than a box.

With shaking hands, I open it.

...2...3...5...7...

Out falls a possum fur willy warmer. Not the exact one that I bought back in New Zealand, but a brand new one still in its wrapping.

A note falls out, and I recognize it as the same piece of paper that I gave to Phillip to pass on to Eric. I hold it up and read it.

You bring me happily ever afters, too. Such as this. While it warms my willy, you were the first thing to ever warm my heart. -E

I chuckle lightly as the tears start falling.

"You know, that was meant to make you laugh, not cry."

I jump at the voice, shrieking in terror as I look up and see...

"Eric?"

The prince grins widely at me. I can't believe it. He's here, standing in my parents' driveway. As if nothing happened.

I look around wildly, trying to figure out where

he came from. "Were you *hiding* in that delivery truck?"

He nods slyly.

"Why?"

He shrugs. "I figured the best way to get your attention was with some grandiose gesture. And I wanted to make you laugh. Especially with what happened back in Dubreva." He wipes away one of my tears with my thumb. "I'm so sorry that happened."

I sniffle. "It wasn't your fault."

"It was," he says. "I should have known that Mother would have tried something crazy."

"She probably just wants to protect her sons and the image of her country."

He shakes his head. "She's a control freak. And, yeah, we're a little unorthodox. But," he pulls me to him, the hard length of his body against mine, "she can't get in the way of who I love."

"I love you, too," I whisper.

I feel his laugh before it bursts from him like sunshine. His lips crash against mine and I lose myself in the kiss. *This*. I thought I'd never get anything like this again.

He breaks the kiss with a grin, his eyes half-lidded as he regards me. "I was so worried I'd never have anything like that again," he murmurs, echoing my sentiments.

"Me too."

"She even threatened to ex-communicate me, you know. Threatened to take everything away from me if I went after you."

I startle, worried for him. "Eric!"

He laughs. "Cara, this is the twenty-first century, not the Dark Ages. Besides, even if she takes my titles and blood rights away from me, I still have all my money. Oh, yeah," he adds at my shocked expression, "I forgot to tell you that most of that was my money. I'll buy you that happily ever after if I have to. But she won't ex-communicate me. I am her son after all."

"What about the scandal?" I ask.

He shrugs nonchalantly. "What do you care what the world thinks. Besides, they're on some other thing right now, about some socialite sex tape." At my skeptical look, he sighs. "Look, Cara, it's not going to be easy. And yeah, the media is going to call us things, things that might not necessarily be true. That I'm your rebound prince, and that you're my revenge to get back at Phillip."

"*That's* what they're saying about us?" I ask with a laugh.

He cups my jaw, stroking the side of my face with his thumb. "So you haven't read anything about that, huh? See, you're already doing fine. And if nothing else, we'll always have a possum fur willy warmer to keep it interesting. Now," I shriek as he picks me up in his arms "I think it's time we escape to somewhere else. What do you say to Rio?"

I laugh as I kiss him back. "Anywhere with you, my prince."

***

Does Phillip get a happy ending? Find out in the next book!

Read on for a sneak peek at the sequel to Erin Hayes's hit The Royal Trade: A Billionaire Prince Romance

READ IT NOW

As the crown prince of Dubreva, Phillip lived a life without regrets. Until now.

Disgraced and humiliated by his very public break-up with his ex- fiancée, Phillip just wants to move on with his life as quietly as a billionaire prince can.

He can't avoid his duties to his people—but he never expected to be thrown into the path of a beautiful CEO who's even more famous than he is. And richer. Not to mention, the media empire she built from the ground up is watching his every move.

Lucky for him, she's not at all interested in helping him find redemption. Then again, Phillip may be falling for her. If only she would stop being such a royal pain.

Read on for a preview

REGRET ISN'T something that crown princes feel often, but after watching my younger brother marry Cara Van Meter, it plows through me like a freight train.

She's up on the dais, looking radiant as she faces Eric, who looks like a smug prick. I say that fondly. I am, after all, the best man. I can't say too many bad things about my younger brother. Especially since he makes her so happy.

You see, I was engaged to her once. Then I fucked up, which made her escape into Eric's arms.

I'm at peace with her decision. No, really, I am. After the way I screwed her over, I'm glad she's moved on, even if it is with him.

But I regret that I can't do a single thing right in my life. Cara may not have been one hundred percent right for me—I know that now—but she made me happy.

Now? Well, now I'm fucking miserable.

We're in the Dubrevian Abbey, surrounded by thousands of people, all holding their collective breaths for the couple's wedding vows. I hear the stifled sobs of a woman in the crowd. I think that's my mother, Queen Victoria, although I can't be certain. She never approved of this marriage. While crying is uncharacteristic for her, Eric going against her express wishes *is* unprecedented.

I stifle my own smile at the thought.

Outside, the streets of our small island nation of Dubreva are filled with my people watching screens and set to cheer when the two kiss. Eric and Cara wanted a small wedding, but my mother stepped in saying that a large wedding would show approval for the union from the crown. In other words, Mother's putting on a show to prove that she's all right with this marriage. She's allowed limited access for the press, although it certainly doesn't feel like it up here with all of the shutters and the attention of an entire country following the proceedings.

This is my country. These are my people, and I should be happy.

Yet I feel like I'm the loneliest man in the world.

Grin and bear it.

It's penance. I'm a cheater. A scoundrel. An asshole. And probably a million other things that the media has called me.

I put us into this mess. I deserve it. All of it.

Right now, as I think about my uptight mother, I'm glad I'm not the only one not having a happy ending.

Yet I still feel...hollow inside.

"These two have given and pledged their life, love and happiness to each other," the bishop proclaims, throwing me back into the present. "And have declared so by giving and receiving these rings. By the joining of their hands, I pronounce that they be husband and wife together, in the name of the Father, and of the Son, and of the Holy Ghost. Amen."

"Does this mean I can kiss her?" Eric asks eagerly.

I fight the urge to roll my eyes, but the bishop's lips curve upwards as she nods. "You may."

Cara laughs as my brother pulls him to her and dips her into a deep kiss as the entire church erupts into cheers. Outside, I'm sure, everyone has seen the kiss and are cheering along with them. It's strange to think that for once I'm not the one in the spotlight. My baby brother is.

I nod, smile, grin and bear it as I keep telling myself.

I'll find my own way.

Seeing my ex-fiancée's brilliant smile, though, makes me wonder if I'll ever have anyone smile at me like that.

I doubt it.

READ IT NOW

DID YOU LOVE THE ROYAL TRADE ?

Reviews help authors out IMMENSELY. In fact, I would call them the biggest help possible.

If you have read *The Royal Trade: A Billionaire Prince Romance,* would you please consider leaving an honest review?

From the bottom of my heart, thank you. Thank you.

ABOUT THE AUTHOR

New York Times Bestselling Author Erin Hayes writes what she wants to read, which includes paranormal romance, contemporary romance, and urban fantasy sprinkled with vampires, billionaire princes, mermaids, steampunk and all the stuff you love.

She lives in San Francisco with her husband and a giant cat, along with too many Sailor Moon figurines and pieces of art she brought back from her travels. When she's not writing, well, she's planning her next big trip or watching sci-fi movies.

And if you like Star Wars, we're already best friends.

Follow her on:
www.erinhayesbooks.com
www.facebook.com/erinhayesbooks
Join her street team at: http://www.facebook.com/groups/erinsnerdcrew/

Made in the USA
Monee, IL
20 December 2025